MAKE ME THE SKY

Make Me the Sky

a novel

Joan Wexler

International Psychoanalytic Books (IPBooks)
New York • http://www.IPBooks.net

Published by IPBooks

The characters and events portrayed in this book are fictitious. Any similarity to real persons, living or dead, is coincidental and not intended by the author.

ISBN: 978-1-956864-44-1

For

Matthew, Sarah, Gabrielle, Rafael, and Elena

Contents

Glossary

Abigail: Girl's name, from Avigail, "My father's joy."

Afikomen: In the Passover ceremony, part of a matzoh is broken off and hidden for the children to find later during the meal.

Bashert: Destiny; also used to indicate a soulmate.

A Beymele: "Young Tree," a Yiddish folk song.

Bris: Covenant; the Jewish rite for circumcision.

A Brivele der Mamen: "A Little Letter to Mama," a Yiddish folk song.

Bubbe: Grandmother.

Chad Gadya: "One Kid." Usually sung towards the end of the Passover ceremony.

Charoses (in Hebrew, Charoset): A ceremonial food for the Passover seder, made of chopped nuts and fruit, sweetened with cinnamon and sweet red wine. Charoses symbolizes the mortar used by the Hebrews to build structures for Pharoah's Egypt.

Cholent: A baked dish usually consisting of meat and beans, prepared ahead for the day of the sabbath.

Chuppah: A canopy under which a bride and groom stand during a marriage ceremony.

Chutzpah: Audacity, nerve.

Daven: To pray with a swaying or rocking motion of the body.

Dayenu: A song sung during the telling of the Exodus at the Passover ceremony. "It Would Have Been Enough" The song praises God for each thing he did to help the Jews escape from Egypt.

Feter: Uncle.

Forverts: The Jewish Daily Forward is an American Newspaper for a Jewish American audience founded in 1897 and published as a Yiddish-language daily newspaper.

Gantse macher: "Big shot," a person of influence.

Get: Divorce.

Haggadah: The word Haggadah means *Telling.* The Haggadah is a text used at the Passover feast, telling about the exodus from Egypt while guiding the ritual of the Seder meal.

Hasid: A member of a strictly Orthodox Jewish sect.

Hashomer: The Watchmen, a Jewish defense organization founded in Palestine.

Kaddish: The Jewish prayer for the dead.

Kugel: a sweet or savory pudding, made with noodles or potatoes, often eaten as a side dish for the sabbath and holidays.

L'Shanah Haba'ah B'Yerushalayim!: Next year in Jerusalem!

Lubavitchers: Members of an Orthodox Hasidic sect.

Makht mir dem himl: "Make me the sky".

Mazel Tov: Good luck or Congratulations.

Meshugana: Crazy person; nonsense, silliness.

Mikveh: Ritual bath.

Minyan: A spiritual community consisting of ten men.

Mitzvah: Good deed, also commandment. *Bar mitzvah* is the coming-of-age ceremony for Jewish males when they turn 13, and also what the new "adult" is called afterwards.

Oy, veh iz mir: "Oh, woe is me."

Payes: Uncut sideburns worn by Hasidic Orthodox men.

Rebbetzin: Rabbi's wife.

Schav: A green borscht made with sorrel.

Schmaltz: Rendered chicken fat.

Schnapps: An alcoholic beverage or liqueur.

Shabes or shabbos (Yiddish): The sabbath. In Hebrew, *shabbat.*

A Shabesdike Zemerl: "A Little Sabbath Song."

Shaina maidel: Pretty girl.

Shiva: Seven-day period of mourning.

Shlof Mayn Kind: "Sleep, My Child." Yiddish lullaby.

Shul: Synagogue.

Shvitz: Steam room, or a steam bath.

Tante: Aunt.

Tateh: Father.

Tefillin: Phylacteries; a pair of small black leather boxes with straps, one for the arm and one for the head, containing scrolls with verses from the Torah. The straps are used to wrap the tefillin around the non-dominant arm and on the head just above the forehead.

Treif: Non-kosher food, such as pork and shellfish.

Tzimmes: A traditional Ashkenazi stew of sweetened vegetables, mostly carrots, with dried fruits such as prunes or raisins, sometimes also with meat. The word also means "a big fuss" in Yiddish.

Yarmulke: Yiddish word for the head-covering or skullcap worn by Orthodox Jewish men, and also by most men when at prayer in a synagogue. Also known as a *kippah* in Hebrew.

Zeyde: Grandfather.

Zumernacht: "Summer Night," a Yiddish folk song.

PART 1

My maternal grandmother, Fannie Selzer, born at the end of the 19th century, came from the Galicia region of Eastern Europe. She lived in a shtetl, a Jewish village, called Bolekhiv, not far from Lviv (now part of Ukraine). One of eight children, she had three older and four younger siblings. When her father fell ill and died, the family became poor. Fannie, at age 15 or 16, was the child chosen to come alone to America to work and send money home to support the family.

When I asked her to tell me stories about herself as a child, she described a lively girl who loved singing, dancing, and rolling down the Carpathian Mountain foothills. The stories stopped there.

Later, I asked her why her mother chose her to come to America. She answered, "Because I was in the middle. The older ones worked and helped at home, and the rest were too young." To me, this seemed like no answer at all.

Questions about her life after arriving in America, she answered perfunctorily. "I lived on the Lower East Side," or "I worked in a factory." I learned nothing about her daily life as a "greenhorn"—she never spoke of her loves, losses, or her Jewish heritage. It was my mother who told me about Fannie's disastrous marriage to a philanderer who deserted Fannie and their three children. My mother, the youngest, was then ten years old.

Around 1943, Fannie sometimes received pale blue airmail letters written in German, with foreign stamps. They all began, "*Liebe* Fannie." I believe her sister sent them. Soon, the letters stopped coming. She never again heard from her mother or siblings. I suspect they perished in the Holocaust.

The Fannie I knew was often fearful. She isolated herself from other people. Several times I heard her say, "Anyone who is not a relative is a stranger." She was often moody or angry. Yet, sometimes, out of nowhere, she became giddy, breaking into song and dance, careening around the apartment. Was this a remnant of the lively child?

Although delicately built, sometimes agile and quick moving, she often needed to lie down or stare out the window. She was predictably unpredictable.

When I began this novel, I intended to write into Fannie's silence, to imagine the stories she didn't tell, and perhaps to understand how Fannie became the woman I knew.

However, as I started writing and imagining young Fannie's letters home as she sailed to America, who she met, and what she observed and recorded in her diary, the Fannie I was writing about took me down her own path. I liked her and didn't want to burden her with my grandmother's brittle nature and bleak life. She became a fictional charter, Fannie Liebermann, who beckoned me to follow her.

As a result, as soon as the Fannie of the story leaves her *shtetl* in Galicia, she and all the characters in the story become entirely fictional. They play their fictional roles against the historical background of Eastern Europe, New York City, and Palestine between the years 1910 and 1919.

Chapter 1: Exodus

Spring 1910

Dear Mama, Aber, Rivka, Yehuda, Esther, Lazar, Kayla, and baby Jacob,

The ship left from Bremen this morning. It is sunny, so I took a walk on the deck. I'm already so lonely without all of you, but now, sitting on my bed and writing to you brings me comfort. Yet I know you will not have this letter until weeks after I reach America.

Mama, you never had the advantage of schooling. The older kids will read my letters to you. I'm so thankful you and *Tateh* allowed me to go to school, all the way to 8th grade. I write better in German than in Yiddish because it was what we learned at school, but I think I'll write as best I can in Yiddish. Some of our Polish neighbors have been mean to us. If any were to get hold of my letters in Yiddish, they surely couldn't read them. So, in Yiddish, I'll freely write about my life in America, and I hope you will all write to me telling all that is happening in our shtetl.

Since that Polish gang, all wearing uniforms, beat Tateh and made him sick, all I can think about is getting to America and earning enough money to bring all of you there.

Mama, you called me a *gantse macher* leaving home to work and send money to our family. I'm too lonely and scared to feel like an important person.

I know you wonder why I didn't stay in Budapest, where you sent me first. For a while, I could send you money from my work in *Feter* Shmuel's grocery store, but things weren't right there. I was frightened and had to get away.

While I'm on this ship, I'm not sending money, but I will again as soon as I start working in New York, America. When Feter Oscar, Tateh's brother, offered to pay my passage to help him with his fish business, I said yes. It was a way to get away from Budapest. I promise someday I'll explain what made it a bad place to stay.

Right now, I'm full of hope life will be good in America. I'm so glad I came home to Bolekhiv to see all of you for a few days before traveling to Bremen to get on board the ship. But the quick visit we had made me miss all of you even more now. Mama, I miss your singing. I miss the Friday smells of baking challah and simmering *cholent*. I have never been so on my own as I am right now. It will be good to be with relatives in New York, even though I've never met them.

It took a while to travel to the ship. As you all know, on Friday morning, big brother Aber took me to Lviv in his cart and horse. When we arrived at Lviv, he left me off at Tante Frieda and Feter Vlad's house. It was hard to watch Aber drive away.

I stayed at Tante Frieda and Feter Vlad's house until Sunday morning. Tante Frieda kept wringing her hands, telling me I looked so thin. I told her, "I'm thin, but I'm strong."

While she cooked for *shabes*, Tante Frieda and I sang Yiddish songs. When she put down her pots and spoons and started to dance, of course, I joined her. We had a great time together. She is a beautiful dancer. It felt like a party.

Mama, you always told me I'm a joyful spirit. I am and so is your sister, Tante Frieda. But being a joyful spirit doesn't keep me from missing all of you.

After the singing and dancing, it was almost sundown. Tante Frieda lit the candles, said the Sabbath prayer, and had ready for dinner a beautiful *schav* with challah and some delicious fish. I spent Saturday with them. We went to *shul*.

On Sunday, we got up very early to go to the railroad station. Tante Frieda gave me a big bundle of food she prepared for the train trip to Krakow. There was so much food, I could share it with a woman and her baby who will meet her husband in New York. He works in a factory and now has an apartment he shares with other families.

The train stopped at Krakow, and I changed trains for Bremen. The train ride from Krakow to Bremen was long and cold. It had snowed heavily, and the train came to a stop in the mountains. We didn't move through the night. All of you gave me enough kronen so when a farm woman came onto the train selling sausages, I bought one. I could only eat a little of it because I think it was *treif*, but Mama, I hope you and the rabbi will forgive me. I didn't want to grow weak on this long voyage. The food on this ship is not Kosher, but I know I must eat. I'm sure it is what you and the rabbi would say. I think it might be difficult to be as observant in America as I was in Bolekhiv.

Have you heard from Tateh since he went up the mountain? I'm terrified I'll never see him again. He looked so sick and sad after the beating he took when the robbers stole his whole payroll at the salt mine. We always worried his job as paymaster was risky. Maybe the mountain air will heal his lungs and his spirit. I hope now he will have time to study Torah. He always wanted to spend his days studying, but he had to work to feed and clothe all of us.

When I get to New York, I'll work hard and try to bring all of you to America soon. I'm so grateful to Feter Oscar. I can't wait to meet him and Tante Goldie and the babies, too. I hope I can earn extra by helping with the babies. I miss baby brother Jacob. He's so smiley, and he makes us laugh. When he starts to talk, write, and tell me what he says.

Mama, you said I was strong and very grown-up for almost 16. I know you're right. I'm the middle child, strong enough to go elsewhere and make more money than I can at home right now. Rivka, you now have a good job at the tanning factory. Aber, you are already known as a skilled carpenter, so you both can earn and help Mama with the family. Mama, you're a wonderful gardener. We're all grateful for our little bit of land, our cow, and the chickens. It will keep the family fed. If there is extra, Rivka and Aber can take it to the market on Sundays.

Esther, dear Esther, my twin, you couldn't take this journey with me because of your heart. We are part of each other. Do you remember how, as little girls, we would braid our hair together, your red hair with my blond hair? Sometimes we braided facing each other, and sometimes with just one braid side to side. Then we'd try to run or skip in perfect time with each other, but before long, one of us would pull the other in a different direction and we'd fall into a pile, giggling the whole time. My greatest treasure is the soft, beautiful blue shawl you knitted for me. I wear it all the time, day, and night. When it gets too warm to wear around my neck, I'll tuck it into the waist of my skirt just to have it with me, to touch and feel you are with me.

Please give a big hug to little Kayla and Jacob. I am so sorry to miss Lazar's *bar mitzvah.*

Love to all of you,

Fannie

I read over my letter and realized something I never thought about before. Mama sometimes complimented Esther and me, like calling me a "*gantse macher*," or a "joyful spirit." She often called Esther "smart." She never complimented the other kids, why only Esther and me?

Two Days later

Dear Family,

I am writing again so soon because it helps me to feel less lonely.

This ship is very big. It's called *The S.S. Neckar*. I sleep in a huge room with many women, and many of them also have children. Things are hard now, but it will be better when I get to America. We'll be there in about 15 days if the ship doesn't meet up with a storm. Lots of people are sick, and it smells horrible.

They set benches up when it is time to eat. We get food, but sometimes the smells are so bad I can't eat. I go up on deck with other girls to get fresh air and drinking water. Sometimes people play accordions and dance. I joined in with some of the other girls. Soon, the girls began to dance with the sailors. I've never danced touching a man before, but I hear it's okay in America. I thought I would try out being like an American. Then a sailor grabbed my hand. I thought he wanted to dance, but he wanted me to go with him some place below the upper deck. He scared me and I pulled away from him. So, if I go up to the deck for air, I keep walking and don't stay long. I try to stay in my bed, called a bunk. It's made of rough wood with a thin straw mattress. The bunks are stacked three high, and I have the top one. I climb up to it with a ladder. It's a little more private, so I'm glad to have it.

Even though it's Spring, it's still cold, so I stay dressed all the time, even when I sleep. I curl up with your shawl, Esther and dream you're in bed with me. When I went to Budapest, it was the first time we were not together both day and night.

Eight Days Later

Dear Family,

I feel better today, but I was sick to my stomach and so weak I couldn't leave my bunk. It's strange because I was fine the first few days. I'm better now.

I made friends with another girl my age who speaks Yiddish. She was taken to the ship's hospital because she had a fever. When I felt sick, I didn't have a fever, so I stayed in my bed except to go to the toilet. The toilet is on the top deck. Down here there are only buckets, and it is disgusting. It's not only the toilets. The floor is covered with filthy straw. There is no linen on the bed. The mattress smells of everybody who ever slept on it. We women try to clean, but we cannot keep up with it. There are too many people. There is no way to stay clean on this ship. I have a small handkerchief I dip in my morning tea and use it to keep a little clean. If I can get up onto the deck, water is available, and I try to wash the handkerchief for the next day.

While I was sick, a friendly sailor brought me soup right to my bunk. It's why I'm better today, but I think I'll just try to stay in bed and sleep a lot to be stronger when the ship reaches America. I'll write some more tomorrow.

The Following Day

Dear Family,

Today is a sad day. One woman on the ship came aboard with a baby, a tiny boy, young enough to need constant cradling in his mother's arms. Soon the baby got sick and cried all the time, but then his crying stopped. Another woman tried to tell the mother the poor little child had died, but the mother only screamed, "No, no, no!" and held even tighter to him. A day passed and one sailor brought the woman to the sick bay. I hear the doctor forcefully pulled the poor dead baby out of the mother's arms. Now we hear the desperate cries of the mother day and night. It is so sad. My heart breaks for her.

I will continue this letter when we get to New York, America.

Seven Days Later

Dear Family,

Our ship stopped a distance from the shore, and we all waited in line to go onto a ferry to Ellis Island. We waited a long time. The rich passengers from the upper decks got on first. My group, the biggest group, is called steerage. We waited a long time because there were so many of us. My rucksack felt heavier and heavier, and my shoulders and back ached. Finally, I got on the ferry with a big crowd of other people. We were crammed together. Suddenly we passed the Statue of Liberty. Everyone cheered, and some of us burst into tears. She is beautiful and stands near the harbor, welcoming all of us with her torch held high and her beautiful gown. She wears a crown and looks like a kind queen who promises to take care of us in America. Mama, I miss you so much. You would have been so gentle when I was sick and brought me tea. But now I feel strong and well again.

Later

I'm finally here at Ellis Island in New York, America. My legs are wobbly as I walk on land after so many days on the ship.

Men in uniform handed us a paper with a number written on it. They kept shouting things I didn't understand. I followed the people, who seemed to know what the men were saying. We had to leave the things we carried in a storage room. I worried I wouldn't find my ruck-sack again. It holds all my warm clothes for winter except your shawl, Esther. I always have it with me.

Soon we entered the biggest hall I have ever seen. We were told to sit and wait on long lines of wooden benches. I thought I was waiting for Feter Oscar to pick me up. But someone explained in Yiddish, we must wait for our health examination. I hope I pass. If you don't pass, you're kept here in the hospital, and if you don't get better soon, you're sent back to where you came from. I feel a little like I want to be sent home, but mostly I want to work and earn money and bring all of you here.

While I was waiting, the husband of the sad mother with the poor dead baby arrived. He went to embrace her. She pushed him away screaming, "Our son is dead. It's your fault, making me come to America on that death ship. I'll never, never forgive you." I don't know if the father even knew his child had died. Was this the way he found out?

What happens to people who die on the ship? One woman told me an old man died in the men's quarters. I must stop writing now. I'm being called in for my health examination.

An Hour Later

I passed the health exam. They sent us to a special room. We climbed a long flight of stairs in single file; we walked through a marked-off area and waited to be seen. They quickly examined our eyes and skin and checked to see if we had a fever. We had to get undressed, which I didn't like. I'm wearing a lot of my clothes, one on top of the other, because it makes less to carry, and it is still cold even though it's Spring.

The eye exam was scary. They have a metal tool like a buttonhook to lift your eyelid and look closely into your eye. The woman next to me spoke German and English. In German, she told me the doctor said I need glasses, but I didn't have any eye disease.

My friend from the boat, her name is Hannah, didn't pass. She had a terrible cough. She will go to the hospital, and if she does not get well soon, she will be sent back home. A doctor wrote a big P on the back of her sweater with chalk. I feel so bad for her and me because we became friends. She is from Lviv. She has a cousin in Bolekhiv, Shaina Wietzner. Mama, do you know the family? Hannah also was supposed to meet her relative. I hoped we could continue our friendship in New York, U.S.A.

A strange woman who seemed very confused and sometimes screamed at night on the ship got the letter X chalked onto her back. She is being sent home right away.

Because I passed my health examination, I went to another room where they asked me many questions. Thank goodness there was a German translator. They asked things like, "Where were you born? Are you married? What is your occupation? Have you ever been convicted of a crime? How much money do you have? What is your destination?" I was worried about the money question because I have only a few kronen with me, but it seemed ok. I said I would live with my uncle, who has a fish business. They were satisfied and let me go.

Finally, I could go into the dining room to eat. I was so hungry. A woman put a bowl of stew in front of me. It was warm and smelled good. It had meat and potatoes and carrots in it. I tried not to eat the meat, in case it was pork, but I only got to spoon up one of the warm pieces of potato when an announcement came over the loudspeaker, "Fannie Liebermann." Then some other English words I couldn't understand. Someone pointed me to the reception area, and Feter Oscar was standing there. He hugged me even though we had never met before. We took a ferry and then a trolley car to where he lives on Eldridge Street.

The trolley ride was not very long. On the way, I saw some of the tallest buildings I've ever seen. Budapest was a big city, but New York is bigger. People here walk fast, and some dress in fancy clothes, clothes we would wear to a wedding. Women wear fancy hats, not babushkas. But as we arrived at Feter Oscar's neighborhood, called "The Lower East Side," people looked much more like our people from home. The buildings are only five stories high here, and the streets are so crowded, people are crushed together. Many are pushing carts and selling food, clothes, dishware, pots, and pans, sewing supplies, and tools. As they move along, they yell out what they are selling. But all this crowd and noise make me happy because people speak Yiddish everywhere. It makes me so excited to work and send you money to come here where we won't have to worry about gangs beating us up because we are Jews. We can all be together here in safe America.

Feter Oscar said little on the trip to Eldridge Street. He resembles Tateh a little, but he has a sterner look.

We got off the trolley and took the short walk to Eldridge Street. It took a while because we needed to push through the crowds.

When we arrived at Feter Oscar and Tante Goldie's building, I saw a beautiful synagogue across the way. My new address is 25 Eldridge Street, so please write when you receive this letter.

We walked up four flights. Many kids were playing on the stairs, and Tante Goldie was at the open door. She stretched out her arms and hugged me very hard and for a long time. Tante Goldie is plump, and when she hugged me close, I couldn't breathe for a moment, but then we sat at her little table in her tiny kitchen, and she had ready some cabbage soup and bread, just like you make, Mama. I closed my eyes and pretended I was home.

Once I was no longer hungry, I realized the commotion of people talking and little kids running around was not only coming from outside but also from inside the apartment. Tante and Feter, I know, have four kids still at home, but then I saw the kids in the next room. There were seven kids and another woman about Tante's age. A man dressed like a *hasid* was bent over his books. Tante explained other people live with them. They are a family of five and sleep in the front room. Tante, Feter, and their four kids sleep in the back room. I was afraid to ask where I would sleep, but then Tante explained I would sleep in the kitchen where we were now. I looked around for a bed. Tante quickly said, "We will put two wooden chairs together and I'll give you two pillows and a quilt."

In Budapest, I slept in a little bed in the back of the store, but here I'll sleep on two chairs. Well, maybe it will always be warmer in the kitchen. I'm young and strong. It probably is no more uncomfortable than the wooden bunks on the ship. Also, I don't think I'll grow any taller, so it should be ok.

Thinking about earning money and bringing all of you here, Tante and I had a conversation. I asked,

"Tante, when can I begin to work at Feter's fish business?" Tante looked confused.

"Fish business, what fish business?" I asked,

"Doesn't Feter have a fish business? He wrote he had a fish business and could sponsor my voyage to America."

Tante was silent for a moment. She closed her eyes and slowly shook her head back and forth. Then opened her eyes and looked straight at me.

"So, he wrote on the form, he had a fish business?"

"Yes"

"No Fannie, there is no fish business. Feter sells old clothes on the street. But there is a lot you can do to make money and bring over your family. Feter needs another set of eyes when he's buying and selling because if he looks away, even for a second, people steal things from his cart. Also, Feter is not good at adding and subtracting; if people speak something besides Yiddish, he can't make out what they're saying. I understand you speak German and Polish."

"Yes," I said, "and Hungarian too."

"You'll be a great help. He'll make more sales, and you'll make some money too. Also, Fannie, I do piecework at home. The coat factory brings me coats. They are all made except for the buttons. I sew them on. If you will help me with the sewing, you'll make a little extra. Now let's put these chairs together. You must be tired after your trip."

I was so tired I fell asleep right away on the two chairs.

Chapter 2: Bondage

Starting right now, I'm keeping a diary. I'll write about everything I see and hear that happens to me in America. I don't have a note-book, and it will be a while before I have the money to buy one. In the meantime, I found neighbors throw away a Yiddish newspaper called *The Forvertz.* I can write on that paper across the printed words until I can buy a notebook. I have a couple of dark pencils.

When I read over the letter to send home, I realized I wrote some things that will make Mama worry. So, I started the letter over, using another of my precious letter-writing papers. I stopped the letter before writing about sleeping on two chairs for a bed and the fish business that doesn't exist.

This diary will be all about my new life, the good and the bad. The letters I'll send home will be news, but not news that worries Mama. Writing whatever I want and only for myself will help to feel less lonely and scared when things don't go well.

Next Morning

Dear Diary,

I woke up this morning to the noise in the street and the family waking up in the front room. Tante was already in the kitchen making tea and cutting bread for breakfast. When Tante looked up and saw me, she said, "Hurry, get dressed. Feter is already saying his morning prayers, and you and he are going out to work."

Feter came into the kitchen, ate, and, without a word, beckoned me to follow him. First, we went into his family sleeping room, and from under the bed, he pulled out two huge potato sack bundles. He handed one to me. "Follow me," he ordered gruffly. I followed him down the four flights of stairs. The bundle was huge, lumpy, and hard to hold without losing my balance. I was sure I'd fall if I didn't go slowly, "Hurry up." he yelled.

On the first floor, from a dark alcove, Feter pulled a dirty quilt off an old baby carriage. I had only seen baby carriages in Budapest. They were for the rich. This one was old and battered, as though someone threw it out. He dumped out his bundle into the carriage and motioned for me to dump mine. This is his pushcart! The clothes were old, faded, and smelly. We went into the street. He started hollering, "Clothes, clothes, clothes for summer and warm clothes for coming cold weather." We moved along when a woman stopped him and began grabbing clothes and throwing them aside. Reaching into the bottom of the baby carriage, she pulled out a child's brown wool coat and started haggling with Feter about the price. Feter poked me in the shoulder and gestured to keep an eye on the stuff in the carriage while he worked out the price with the woman. In the meantime, a man came by, dug out a pair of old black shoes, and started to haggle with Feter while he was still doing business with the woman. Their voices were getting louder and louder.

"This coat has a torn lining," the woman complained. "Twenty cents, not another penny."

"These shoes have no laces," shouted the man. "I'll give you ten cents for them. They are not even worth that."

"Twenty-five cents," screamed Feter.

They went on like this while Feter stubbornly yelled a higher price. I could see why he needed someone to keep an eye on the carriage full of clothes. Finally, the man and woman each settled on a price for the shoes and the coat. Feter kept his money in a dirty cloth bag with a string around his neck. We kept going through the streets. People leaned out the windows yelling to Feter:

"Show me a man's jacket."

"My boy needs a pair of pants."

Feter rummaged through the pile, and if he held up something they might want, they came down to the street to look closely.

Later that day, a kid ran by the carriage fast, grabbed something from the cart, and ran away. I tried to run after him. I'm a fast runner, but he got away. Feter screamed and shook his fist,

"You lazy, stupid girl. If it happens again, you'll pay for what's lost."

Even though I would never tell Mama about this, I felt lonelier than I have since leaving Bolekhiv.

The day went on like this. We returned to the apartment at noon for barley soup and bread, then went out again until supper. Feter thought he had a good day except for the stolen garment.

The other family had already eaten, and now Tante, Feter, the kids, and I sat down to pot cheese, noodles, and tea. I was so hungry, and still hungry after all the food was gone.

After we ate, Feter made me sit with him at the table. He counted the money and then told me what he had paid for the old clothes.

"So, Fannie, how did I make out?"

"Feter, you made one dollar and 20 cents." He scowled at me.

"I came out better than that." He growled. He recounted the money and snapped,

"So, tell me my profit."

"Sorry, Feter, but it's the same as before." He sneered,

"You must be very stupid, or else you pocketed the money. Show me your pockets!" he screamed.

When he saw I had no pockets, he screamed at me to take off my clothes. I ran out of the house. He tried to chase me, then stopped and just cursed me. I didn't know where to go, so I sat on the stoop, tears pouring down my face, and finally went back into the apartment. Where else could I go? Tante must have heard all this, but she stayed silent in their sleeping room.

I was very tired, but as soon as Feter and the kids went to bed, Tante sat down at the table with her coats, buttons, needles, and thread and showed me how to sew the buttons onto the coats. There was a stack of coats and a bag full of buttons. She told me, "They will pick up these coats in the morning, so be sure to finish before you go to sleep."

Finally, I finished. I put together the two wooden chairs with the pillows and the quilt and sobbed until sleep overtook me.

The days went on like this for another week. Thank goodness no one stole anything from the carriage. But Feter kept shouting, "I thought you're supposed to be smart, that you could add and subtract. I see you can't. How did I get stuck with such an idiot?"

I got better at sewing buttons and at least could go to sleep earlier than that awful first night.

Dear Diary,

It thrilled me to get a letter from Mama, but the news is not good. She probably dictated it to Rivka. She wrote:

"It's harder and harder to buy anything because the price of everything is so high. I'm so glad I decided not to sell any of the little land we have. It

is more necessary than ever to grow our own vegetables. Our cow is still giving some milk. A few of the chickens are laying eggs. So, we are doing better than neighbors who have no land. We have enough clothes for this winter. I hope things will improve. Gangs are still roving, but they seem to have moved on to other shtetls for now."

I suspect things are harder than Mama writes. I'm not letting her know all that I'm going through. I wonder if she's also leaving out bad things happening to them.

Later in her letter, Mama brought up something she had never said. *"Fannie, you should think about getting married. It might make things safer for you. You can continue to work in Feter's fish business until you have a baby. Then, like Tante, you can do piecework at home."*

How does she know I don't feel safe? Maybe she guessed what happened in Budapest.

I have no interest in getting married now. And I certainly don't think I should get married before Rivka. Tateh tried to make a match for Rivka before he was beaten, but the other family didn't think her dowry was big enough. And what can I offer a husband? I'm a poor greenhorn who must find some way to get enough money to bring over my family. But so far, neither Feter nor Tante has given me any of my earnings. I'll ask Tante tomorrow. I'm afraid to ask Feter until he trusts me more.

Two Weeks Later

Dear Diary.

After sewing buttons every night for two weeks, I asked Tante about earnings to send home. She sat straight up, and for the first time, she sounded harsh. "Fannie, you should be ashamed. You have a roof over you, and you eat with us. You don't yet earn enough to cover your share of the rent or the food you eat. You'll get paid when you have earned what we put out for your ticket to come to America and what we put out for your food. You're an ungrateful girl. I don't want to hear from you about your earnings again. Feter and I will let you know when you start earning more than what it costs us to keep you and what we paid to get you here."

It shocked me to hear Tante's angry words. But then I saw Feter hovering just on the other side of the door. Is Tante afraid of her husband? Maybe she is. After she heard him leave the apartment, she came up to me while I was cleaning the kitchen, and with her finger over her lips, she handed me a piece of bread with *schmaltz*. I need money, not bread and schmaltz!

I don't know what to do if I don't start earning. Did Mama think this could happen? Is that why she brought up getting married? Does she think I need someone to watch over me? No, I don't want a husband. I want my family.

Dear Esther, my beloved twin,

I'm so lonely I must spill my heart out to someone I love. I know I have hinted that something bad happened in Budapest. I don't want Mama to know what happened, but I need someone who cares about me to know. We always kept secrets together and told each other everything. I hope we can still do that through letters. You, Mama, and I were entwined together from the moment our life began, even before being born into the world. You and I are both different and the same. We look alike, like sisters do, but not exactly alike. You came into the world with a delicate heart. I came with a twisted leg. My leg got better by dancing every day. I hope your heart stays well by resting a lot. We both loved to read, but I think you may become a real scholar. I know you have been studying Hebrew. Wouldn't that be wonderful, a woman scholar. If we hadn't lived in Austria, we would never have been able to go to school.

I'm unburdening myself, but dear Esther, please know that I have learned a lot and know better how to take care of myself, so please don't let this burden you. Please, just let it be part of our bond. Here is my secret.

Soon after arriving in Budapest, Feter Shmuel's grocery store had to close. Gentiles stopped going there because it was a Jewish business. Feter tried selling on the street, but nobody would buy from him because of his beard and *yarmulke*. Jews didn't buy because they feared if they were seen doing business with Feter Shmuel, it would identify them as Jewish, and they'd be harassed. There are roving gangs in Budapest like those that beat our poor Tateh.

The family in Budapest resented me. I was another mouth to feed and not able to work. Then one terrible day, Feter Shmuel brought me to an older woman who lived with a bunch of young women in a respectable-looking big apartment building. Esther, it was a brothel. Feter was trying to make a deal with the woman to sell me into her business. I was so shocked. She wanted me to take off my clothes, and when I was reluctant, Feter slapped me hard. So, I did. Feter Shmuel told the woman I could dance and sing. I wanted to run away, but I couldn't run naked.

Feter put his hands around my throat and demanded I sing and dance. So, I did. I have never been so scared or embarrassed. They made a deal. Feter asked for a price and the woman bargained down. Then Feter walked out with his money, leaving me at the brothel.

Someday, I will tell you how I escaped and somehow convinced Mama to contact Feter Oscar in America. Maybe he could use an extra pair of hands in his fish business. By the way, it is not a fish business but an old clothes business. He doesn't even own a pushcart but sells the clothes from an old baby carriage someone threw away. You must keep that a secret too.

Mama may not know how to read and write, but she is smart. I wonder if she hasn't realized that something bad happened in Budapest. Recently, she suggested I might get married. Esther, I don't want a husband. I only want you and Mama.

Lots of love to you,

Fannie

Three weeks later

A letter arrived from Esther.

"Dear Fannie,

What a shocking thing to happen to you. I'm so relieved to know you found your way out of Budapest, and I hope America, with time, will become good to you. Of course, we have our bond, and I will keep your secrets in my heart as we have always done for one another.

Yes, at night when everyone is asleep, I continue to try to read Hebrew. I open some of Tateh's books and become knowledgeable. We were always the curious ones in our family. I have been wanting to read Hebrew and Torah since I learned to read. And you loved reading too. Not religious texts, but any book you could find. You often borrowed books from the richer girls at school, and sometimes our teachers loaned you books. I remember you sitting in the apple tree reading and I would have to call you many times before you heard me. You were so absorbed. My reading Hebrew is my secret to you. The rabbi would be angry to know a girl tries to read Hebrew and has the chutzpah to consider herself capable of being scholarly.

But dear Fannie, here is another much harder secret to tell you. My heart is growing weaker. I spend much of the day in bed because I so quickly get out of breath. I feel badly I cannot even help watch the little ones. I'm no help to the family. Our family is getting poorer, and I am just another mouth to feed. I tried to watch baby Jacob, but then he crawled too fast to the edge of the stairs. I caught him in time and then almost fainted with the effort. Mama must see I'm growing weaker. She says nothing, and neither do I. She sent for the doctor once. He told me to stay in bed as much as possible, and then I heard him reassure Mama that I would get well again, but he did not reassure me. He is a kind man. When he examined me, he sighed. I think he caught himself mid-sigh and frowned as though he was only concentrating harder. I don't want to burden you. You have your own burdens to bear now. Please know I feel great relief and even strength in writing to you honestly about what is happening to me.

Your loving twin,

Esther

Dear Diary,

I'm so worried about my Esther. I can't bear the thought she could die, another reason to bring the family here soon. Maybe Esther first, so she can get care at an American hospital.

Still no wages. It's been three weeks. But right now, earning is not the big worry. Three times I woke up at night, and Feter stood over me and stared down at me. When he saw me open my eyes, he ran like a rat to his room. Then later, he snuck back in and whispered in my ear, "You want to get paid? I'll show you how to get paid." He clamped his hand over my mouth and then stuck his hand under the quilt and tried to grab my woman parts. "If you scream, I'll say I caught you trying to steal food from the kitchen."

What am I going to do? Is this what happens to all unmarried girls who leave home? Coming to America seemed like a chance to make everything right, and it's as bad as it ever was. What can I do? I can't burden poor Esther with another terrible secret. I'm so alone.

Dear Diary,

At dawn, I went out into the street before everyone else was up. It was a blessing. It must have been G-d's will. Down the street comes Hannah, my friend from the ship. I threw my arms around her, and we hugged for a long time. Finally, I asked, "What happened to you?"

"They were afraid I had tuberculosis because I was coughing so much, but I only had pneumonia, so after a week in the hospital, they let me go. It didn't work out with my sponsor, so I had to find a job for myself. Someone told me they needed basters in a dress factory. Then I needed a place to stay. I heard the Young Women's Christian Association had housing for new immigrants, so I borrowed a cross from an Italian friend and spoke only German. I stayed there for a while. Then I met some of the other girls from the factory. They invited me to live with them on Essex Street and help with the rent. We have one room, and there are five of us, but it's okay."

When I asked what happened with the family sponsoring her, she started crying. "I ran away. The family tried to make me a match with a smelly old man willing to pay for a wife." I told her,

"My sponsor, my uncle, refuses to pay me for the work I'm doing day and night."

"Fannie, maybe you can get a job in the factory where I work. I'll ask. I'm on good terms with the supervisor." We hugged again, and Hannah walked on to her job.

How can I work in a factory when I have no place to live except here in this apartment with Feter and Tante and everyone else? I can't even pay for the Young Women's Christian Association. It's getting warm now. Maybe I can sleep in the street until I figure it out. I see plenty of people who seem to live in the street and beg. What am I thinking! I'm desperate, even more desperate than I knew. But I must get away from Feter. He is keeping me like a slave. He's a monster. Even Tante is his slave. Do I have to feel grateful to him for getting me to America, to be his slave?

Dear Diary,

Hannah and I planned to meet again early the next morning before she started her day at the factory. I met her on Essex Street in front of her building where she lives in a tiny room with four other women. Hannah pointed out the fire escape outside of her window. She thinks I could climb up there at night in the warm weather. Lots of people, she says, sleep on the fire escape in the summer. She said she could bring me food and keep my belongings under her bed. They always close the curtain, so the landlord won't see me if he enters the room. Maybe in summer, I can do this. Hannah is trying to be kind. If I begin earning a little, I can pay rent.

What a good friend Hannah is. She makes me feel lucky even when life is so hard. And I can keep finding discarded copies of the *Forvertz*. Writing keeps my spirits up almost as much as singing and dancing. Will I ever sing and dance again?

Oh no! Mama will send her letters to Eldridge Street. How can I explain I'm moving to a fire escape on Essex Street? She'd have a fit! No, I won't tell her about the fire escape. And then what will I do if it rains? I must find somewhere to live.

Dear Mama,

I am so sorry to say that Feter and Tante have put me to work, but they say they can't pay me because first I must make up to them the cost of my passage and the food they provide for me every day. This isn't why I came all the way to America. Mama. I need to earn to bring you and the family here. Do you have any other relatives in New York who can give me a place to stay? I think I can get a regular paying job in a dress factory. Hannah, my friend from the ship, works there and is recommending me.

Love to you and to all our family,

Fannie

Weeks Later

Finally, a letter from Mama in Rivka's handwriting.

"Dear Fannie,

I'm shocked and angry your Tateh's brother is making you work and not paying you. He has a fish business, for goodness's sake. He probably makes plenty of money. Your Tateh would be so ashamed of his brother.

My young cousin Itzhak and his wife, Sadie, are on Pike Street. If they think your stay is only for a while, they will be more likely to take you. You should offer to pay them something from what you earn at the factory. I will write to him.

Fannie, I mean it when I say you should think of getting married. Itzhak could arrange a match for you. I'll write to him about that too."

Mama sounds so angry and worried about me. And she only knows half of it.

Chapter 3: Thou Shalt Not...

Summer 1910

Dear Diary,

I hate Feter Oscar. I thought I hated Feter Shmuel for trying to sell me to a brothel, but I hate Feter Oscar even more. He is disgusting. When he wasn't yelling at me or trying to touch me, he was staring at me. I wanted to disappear.

I ran away from Eldridge Street and slept on Hannah's fire escape. Now I live with Mama's cousin Itzhak and his wife, Sadie, in a tiny apartment on the fifth floor on Pike Street. The bigger room, which is very small, has a sofa and the kitchen. Sadie and Itzhak have a bedroom, barely bigger than a cupboard, holding only two narrow beds.

I work in the same factory as Hannah. My life has improved. I get paid and can send a little money home. I should be pleased but I'm tormented.

Diary, what I must tell you is painful to write. I wish I could die. I wish I had Esther's frail body and could give her my strong one. I can't stand myself. I think I'm going crazy. I hope writing it helps. I'm a thief! There it is. I wrote it. I'm a thief! I'm a thief! I'm a thief! Feter Oscar called me a thief. And now I am a thief.

The night I ran away, I went to his repulsive baby carriage, plunged my hand into that mess, and from the bottom of that stinking pile, I stole a dress. It was the first thing I grabbed, and then I ran. I don't need it. It's too big for me. I enjoyed the revenge for a moment, but then I was horribly scared and guilty. I could go to prison or be sent home if I'm caught. I wish I could go home, but not as a shameless criminal. I stuffed the dress into the bottom of my rucksack and put it all under the sofa where I sleep on Pike Street. My family would be so ashamed of me. I've become filth, and I see filth everywhere here in America.

It is summer and very hot. The smell of rotting garbage and all the human smells are everywhere. The streets are full of horse manure, not all the streets are paved, and when it rains, while it relieves the heat sometimes, walking through the streets is revolting. We had plenty of mud in our shtetl, but it didn't also stink of garbage and human bodies. In the building, the rats run wild. When climbing the stairs, I must stamp my feet. I must stamp my feet again on each flight until I reach the fifth floor. I can't even describe the state of the outhouse in the yard. It's as bad as the ship. I hear rats in the apartment at night and have even seen them on the windowsill and, yes, even on the table.

The Statue of Liberty does not care for us like a gentle mother. We had some of the same troubles at home, but there was clean mountain air. I had my family and a clean conscience. I wasn't yet a common thief.

When I go out onto the street, I look for Feter Oscar. Once, he caught sight of me and started cursing. I know he wanted to grab me, but he was too afraid to leave his stupid baby carriage. I keep a lookout for him. If I see him at a distance, I run for it, scurry like a rat. He's convinced I cheated him and stole money. I did steal, and he deserved it. But I'm scared of him, scared of what could happen to me, and scared of shaming my family. I can't stand myself. He doesn't know where I live, but it's only a matter of time before he finds out. Does he realize the dress is missing?

Diary, I can barely sleep, but I have awful dreams when I do. I dreamed Feter Oscar discovered the missing dress. In the dream, it was night, I was on the street, and he jumped out of a door, grabbing me. I can't even tell you, Diary, what he tried to do. I woke up screaming, and Sadie rushed in. I told her I was dreaming of Tateh being beaten. Now I'm a liar too. What am I turning into? Mama was so proud of me. It would horrify her to know what I've become. There's no one to talk to about this. I must tear up what I just wrote. No one can know my disgusting secrets. Esther is such a good soul, and she's so frail. I'm scum, but somehow, I survive in filth and have become filth.

Diary, I was about to rip up what I wrote when I saw that the *Forvertz* has an advice column called *A Bintel Brief*.[1] Some people write in and don't give their names. One letter reads,

"Dear Bintel Brief,

I came to America to escape pogroms and poverty. Now in America, I find only poverty and brutality. I am a religious man and wear the garb of the Hassid. I live in New Jersey, where some of my family settled. I cannot tell you how many times they have taunted me on the streets as I try to find work, going from store to store, factory to factory. I have no skills except to be knowledgeable of Torah. The worst moment happened yesterday. It was evening, and I was returning to where I live after a day

---

1 Metzker, Isaac. *A Bintel Brief (A Bundle of Letters): Sixty Years of Letters to The Jewish Daily Forward.* New York: Schocken Books, 1971.
   (All letters that appear to and from *A Bintel Brief* are fictional but are written in the style of *A Bintel Brief*.)

of no success finding work. Suddenly, three thugs pushed me against a wall.

One had a scissor. He cut off my payes and part of my beard. The three of them ran, but I caught the guy with the scissors and threw him to the ground. He was a small skinny kid, but I didn't care. I punched his face over and over until I heard a crack, and his nose gushed blood. I think I broke his nose and knocked out his teeth. He screamed in pain. The others ran away, and so did I. But I stopped, ran into a doorway, and looked out at the kid lying on the ground. I was afraid I killed him. Soon he moved and got up. He was crying and holding his face, but thanks to G-d he was alive.

I am horrified that I drew blood and could have murdered him. I'm not a violent man, but I fear that I have encountered violence in America and have myself become violent. I am filled with hatred for those who have treated me with cruelty. I have become cruel myself and filled with self-hatred as well. I left my home in Russia to find peace. I find no peace in America. Dear Bintel Brief, please help me change. I can't bear what I have become."

Here is the answer A *Bintel Brief* wrote back.

"Dear Religious Man of Greatly Disturbed Conscience,

When we poor humans are brutally humiliated, if we have a life force left, we fight—sometimes to our detriment, and sometimes we do real harm. It is part of our human nature, albeit a sad part. The attack on your person by this young thug was not only a physical assault, but an attack on your deep identity as a religious man. I suggest you go to the synagogue nearest you and ask to speak with the chief rabbi. I believe that while he will not condone your attack on this boy and beating *him, he will be moved by your recognition, that you also are capable of brutality. I suspect he has heard of many cases where men who wear religious garb are taunted and beaten. Hopefully, he will help you deal with this sad situation that happens not only where we escaped from but even here in America, this so-called 'Land of the Free.'"*

Diary, I am touched by the compassion shown in answer to this poor man. I wrote my letter. Here it is. Of course, I'll send it without my name.

Dear *Bintel Brief*,

I am around 16 years old from a shtetl in Galicia. My family is poor, so my mother sent me first to Budapest and now to America to live with relatives, work, and send money home. Two male relatives have treated me poorly. In Budapest, my relative tried to sell me to a brothel. I escaped. My mother then sent me to America to work for my uncle. He made me work without pay unless I allowed him forbidden use of my body. I was frightened, but also angry. I ran away, but first, I stole something from him. I never stole before, but I wanted to do something hateful. I ended up hating myself for becoming a thief. I don't need what I stole. It is useless to me. I cannot throw it away. I feel so guilty I keep it hidden to remind myself to never do such a shameful thing again. If my family knew I was a thief, it would mortify them. This is haunting my dreams. I feel so repulsed by what I have become. With help from some good people, my life situation has now improved. I now work in a factory, get paid, and can even send a little money home to my struggling family in Europe. My mother writes how proud she is of me, yet I feel like filth. Please help me so I can go on living with myself.

A few days my letter was answered.

"Dear Haunted,

When you write you feel like 'filth,' it is a sad state you have come to. Two relatives treated you poorly, and you did something that now invites you to treat yourself poorly. Yes, it is wrong to steal, but in the wrongs that we humans can inflict on each other, this is not irreparable. Since this relative was intent on putting you in danger, I advise you not to return whatever you stole. I suggest you consider giving this stolen article to someone who can make good use of it. While it does not erase your theft, it is an effort to give something good instead of a wrong taking.

I hope the improvement in your life situation is soon matched by relief from your inner turmoil."

Dear Diary,

I did what *A Bintel Brief* suggested. On Sunday, I took the stolen dress to the public baths, and there I washed and ironed it and repaired the torn seams. I found some thrown-out brown paper, wrapped it up, and took it to the post office, where I had it sent home. It will fit Mama. Now I can sleep, although I still feel ashamed for getting my revenge by becoming a thief. I feel better putting it to good use for someone I love and who needs it.

If Mama knew how I came by it, she would get rid of it and probably get rid of me, too.

Chapter 4: The Work of Our Hands

A few weeks later

Dear Diary,

I'm settling in with Cousin Itzhak and his wife, Sadie. They are good people. I like them. Itzhak is quiet, very religious and doesn't work except to read Torah and Talmud. Sadie works in a hat factory sorting and cleaning feathers. Sadie and Itzhak are older than me but still young, maybe 19 or 20. Sadie yearns to be a mother. She tells me she worries that she has not yet gotten pregnant. If she doesn't have a baby soon, she fears Itzhak may divorce her so he can find a wife who will bear him children.

Sadie tries to take care of me. She always asks if I eat anything during the day and tells me I'm too thin. She wants me to get a good rest at night on her sofa and lets me use a wonderfully soft puffy quilt she brought from Poland. It was her quilt when she was a child. I'm small, so it covers me perfectly.

I started working at the factory a couple of weeks ago. It's a huge building, covering most of a city block. I had heard of elevators, and now I ride one every day to the 8th floor. There are several elevators. Some are for freight and some for the workers. The one I use is run by a man who makes it go by pushing a handle forward in a half-circle groove, then pulling it back when we stop at a floor. Every time it starts, I think my stomach will leap up and out of my mouth. When the elevator stops, my stomach comes heaving back down. I was told you get used to it, but that hasn't happened yet. I wish I could use the stairs. We're not allowed to take the stairs. They keep the doors to the stairways locked. I think it's so they can see us coming and going using the elevator, and not sneaking out down the stairs when we're supposed to be working. It also means we can't even take the time to pee, except on our lunch break. I finally got up my nerve to ask Sadie what she does about this problem at the hat factory. She told me to drink only a half cup of tea in the morning, put layers of rags in my underwear as though I'm having my monthlies, and then try to hold it all day. Older women have a harder time holding it. But they don't have to worry about their monthly. Sadie's advice is good. I won't embarrass myself. I'll also be ready for that time of the month.

Before I asked Sadie what she does, I had an embarrassing experience. I was at my workstation, and I realized my monthly had started. How could I stand up at the end of the day without everyone seeing what happened? Then I remembered I had Esther's blue shawl tucked into the band of my skirt. I tied it around my waist when I stood up, so no one would notice anything. Thank you, Esther. You helped me!

All these things would be more manageable if I did piecework at home, but I earn more at the factory and get to know more people. We are mostly Jewish and Italian women. So far, the Jewish women stick together, and so do the Italian women. Maybe that will change when we all get more confident talking English. It's a hard language to learn.

We have ten minutes to eat something midday. In the beginning, I brought a big piece of bread. Sadie insists I also bring some herring or cheese. Sadie is such a good person. She wants a baby so much. I hope someday she will be a mother.

On the 8th floor where we work, we sit in rows. There are rows and rows of women of all ages. Some are even younger than me, and some could be my grandmother. It's not really a dress factory. We make something called shirtwaists, a special kind of woman's blouse that fits snugly and has puffy sleeves. Some women use sewing machines. They make a little more money. As a newcomer, I sew on buttons. I had plenty of practice with Tante's coats, but these are tiny buttons in a long straight row down the shirtwaist's front or back. I hope I'll have enough extra money to buy a shirtwaist someday.

Shirtwaists cost almost one dollar. They sell them in stores. At home, we don't sell clothes in stores. We buy the cloth and sew ourselves.

You can tell who a greenhorn is by what we wear. Greenhorns still wear the clothes they wore in Europe, plain long skirts, and blouses in dark colors. Women who find their place in America wear light-colored shirtwaists.

In the factory, we sit very close and must work fast. They pay us for each job we finish. I hope someday I can learn to work with a sewing machine to make more money. But the machines can be dangerous. The women sometimes get their fingers caught under the needle. They wrap up their fingers with scraps of cloth and keep working because it's rush, rush, rush to finish each job and quickly start the next. But if blood gets on a shirtwaist, they are fined for it.

At first, I was so tired at the end of the day from working at the factory, I was even too tired to write a letter home or write in this diary. It's getting a little better. I'm getting used to it.

The first week, I earned three dollars. I sent one dollar home, gave one dollar to Sadie for rent, and used one dollar for food for Itzhak, Sadie, and myself. When Mama received the dollar, Rivka wrote to say she was as joyful as she had ever seen her, and proud of me. When I brought the dollar to the money changer here, he said everything at home costs more than it ever did. But now, an American dollar is like two or even three dollars at home. I felt good about it. At least I'm helping a little. But I don't think I'll earn enough to pay for even one passage. What will happen to Esther? How can I go on without my twin?

Mama said I should not worry about earning enough to bring them to America. It's enough to send them a dollar a week. She wants to find another sponsor and send the boys so they can avoid the military. She again writes that I should get married, and she wants Itzhak to arrange a match. She must still be worried about me. I still worry about Feter Oscar coming after me. I try not to think about him and to keep going with my life. Long working days take my mind off my troubles, and when I get home, I'm so tired. I have something to eat and go to bed. I have no trouble sleeping anymore. My life is better now. I still long to be with my family, especially Mama and Esther, but living with good people and beginning to find some friends helps a lot with loneliness.

There is one more thing about working at the factory. We must work part of the day on Saturday, so I can't keep the Sabbath. Maybe that is another reason Mama wants me to get married and earn by doing piece-work at home.

When I talk to some of the older girls at the factory who are also away from their families, I hear they become less and less religious. They don't worry about keeping kosher. They like to dance the American way, where you touch your partner. One Jewish girl is in love with an Italian boy!

Chapter 5: Song of Songs

Mid-Summer 1910

Dear Diary,

The factory is noisy and crowded, and the work is hard, but I look forward to going every morning, because I meet Hannah on the way. It gives us a chance to talk, and then we meet again at the end of the day. Hannah still lives with four other women. She seems to have extra money. Maybe she is doing some piece work at night. She bought herself a couple of shirtwaists and goes to movies and the Yiddish theatre. Hannah always loved acting, dancing, and singing and dreams of being an actress on the Yiddish stage. On her day off, she dresses up and goes to American dance halls. She learned some American dances and hopes someone from the theater will see her dancing and think she is talented and pretty. She goes out with men and has asked me twice if I would like to meet someone, a friend of a man she knows. I'm not ready for that, but I did say to Hannah that I noticed a young man working at the factory who speaks Yiddish. He repairs sewing machines and teaches the women to operate them. Hannah knew who I meant.

"That's Mischa. You're not the first girl to notice him. The girls talk about him a lot and we tell each other what we find out about him. He came from a shtetl in Russia with his father a year ago. He has a married sister and two older brothers who are still in Russia. The brothers moved to a city and worked as merchants. They were doing all right until a pogrom came through the town and destroyed the shop. Mischa wants to get the family out of Russia as soon as he can. Now his father repairs shoes, working from their apartment."

I asked, "What happened to his mother?"

"I think she died just before they left. I don't know what she died of."

Diary, I have never spoken to Mischa. He is handsome, tall, with curly black hair and shining brown eyes. He's clean-shaven. Hannah says he is Jewish but not religious and may be a freethinker. She also thinks he's a Zionist. She overheard him talking to another young worker, saying he wants most in the world to move to Palestine and create a Jewish nation. I wonder how his father feels about that.

Weeks later

Dear Diary,

I haven't written to you in awhile, but I am so excited by what happened tonight, I'm bursting. Hannah goes to a place called a settlement house. She is learning English there, and she wants me to come with her and join her class. I'm reluctant. What if I can't learn English? Then she said, "Even if you don't come to the class, come with me on Sunday afternoons. We meet people our age. Sometimes they have a musician, maybe a clarinet player, and we sing Yiddish songs."

I asked, "So, women sing in front of men?"

"Oh yes," she said, "We all sing together."

Dear Diary,

I agreed to go to the settlement house. I hope Mama would understand. I'm not sure she would, but I couldn't resist the chance to sing Yiddish songs. Cousin Sadie encouraged me to go. She said I am still young and need to be with people my age. I worried about my clothes and clumsy old boots. Sadie is sure I will look no different from most other girls there.

So, Diary, I went. Before walking through the door, I decided to unbraid my hair. I think my long blond hair is my best feature. As soon as I felt my hair fall over my back, I was less worried about my plain country clothes.

I felt shy, but went in and searched for Hannah. She was talking to a boy but turned to greet me.

Soon it was singing time, and who do you think was the musician for the night? It was Mischa from the factory. He played the fiddle and accompanied us while we sang all the songs Mama and Rivka taught me. When we sang *Zumernacht*, I couldn't stop the tears, but I was not the only one. Then I was in tears again with *A Beymele*. Esther and I always sang that together. After that, Mischa played Hungarian czardas and Polish mazurkas.

I couldn't help myself. I had to get up and dance. Soon others did too. It felt like I was at home again, lost in sheer joy. I looked up, and Mischa was right there, playing his fiddle and doing the steps with me. I can't remember feeling so excited and joyful. And if that wasn't enough, after the dancing stopped, he asked if I would like to step outside for a breath of air. We did. As soon as we were alone, he seemed shy.

Then he said, "You're a wonderful dancer. I hope to see you here again. I come here on Sundays. I don't always play my fiddle; I fill in if they need someone. This is a good place, and the people who come are nice."

Diary, I felt happy all over, from the tips of my toes to the ends of my hair. I wanted to dance again right there in the street. I could only nod and squeak out, "Yes, I'll come back."

Then he said, "See you tomorrow at work." I didn't think Mischa had ever noticed me.

All this week at the factory, I kept looking at Mischa. Then he might look back at me, and of course, I pretended I was only looking at my buttons.

The following Sunday, I went back to the settlement house. The program was different. They had a teacher showing us greenhorns how to do the American dances where men and women dance together, touching each other. Hannah was helping me to learn the steps when Mischa came up to us. I thought he would ask me for a dance, but oh Diary, he didn't. Instead, he had the *chutzpah* to ask, "Hannah, will you dance the waltz with me?"

It was like an ice pick plunged into my stomach. It was horrible. I didn't expect to feel so much pain. Why do I feel so badly just because a boy I like asked to dance with my one good friend in America? I was so sure he was going to ask me to dance. Didn't he dance the Mazurka and the Czardas with me last week? Was he being Jewish last week and American this week? I hurt so much, and I can't tell Hannah, and I can't write Esther about this either, when her own pain is so much worse.

Hannah and I didn't talk at all on our way home. She went to Essex Street, and I went back to Pike Street. Diary, as I closed the door, I sobbed, curled up on the sofa, and wrapped myself in Esther's shawl.

Esther, I can't bear the thought of losing you. All this sadness makes me want to find some way to go home. There is no way to go home. I have no money for a ticket. All I can do is wrap myself up in your beautiful soft blue shawl and imagine we are children, curled up in our bed, holding each other on cold nights in Bolekhiv.

Dear Diary,

How did I get through the night? Maybe Esther's shawl gave me enough comfort to bear it.

This morning, Hannah and I met on our way to the factory. Hannah was upset, too. She didn't seem at all interested that Mischa asked her to dance. She hoped for a man she knew from the dance hall, Saul, to seek her out, but he paid her no attention. I, of course, didn't say what was on my mind, but I think Hannah knew. She should have refused to dance with Mischa when he asked her. Isn't it what a good friend does? But how can I be all upset about such things when my family in Europe is struggling, and my twin sister may be dying?

Dear Diary,

I have so much to tell you. After that Sunday at the dance, as I expected, Mischa paid no attention to me for days. On Monday, I sat sewing but was crying inside and trying to keep up with the work. The days passed slowly. I stopped being angry with Hannah. I think she was wrong, but maybe she was upset about Saul and wanted Saul to see her dancing with another boy. And besides, I need a close friend here in America. I can't let myself be too angry with Hannah.

Finally, on Thursday, the end-of-the-day bell rang. As I walked out of the factory, my eyes met Mischa's. He was standing there in the street, and when he saw me, he rushed over. At first, he didn't say anything. Then he stuttered, and—I couldn't believe it—he had tears in his eyes.

"Fannie, please forgive me. I've been so sad all week, and I can't help but see that you look sad. You usually talk to the girls who work beside you, but your head was down the whole time this week. Seeing you so sad gives me the courage to talk to you. I wanted to ask you to dance with me at the settlement house, but I was so scared you would refuse to do an American dance with me. I know you are a religious girl, and I have the reputation of being non-religious and a freethinker. I was so afraid you would refuse me...so afraid that at the last second, I was a coward and asked Hannah instead."

Diary, I couldn't believe what I was hearing. I burst into tears right there. Mischa took both my hands in his, then put his hands on my shoulders. Dear Diary, I fell into his arms, and we both sobbed. I was sobbing for joy, for loneliness, for homesickness. I didn't have to say more. Mischa asked if I would spend time with him and dance at the settlement house. I couldn't talk. I nodded, and he took out his handkerchief, dried my tears, and even told me to blow my nose while he held his handkerchief to my face. Diary, I was so comforted by his words and, yes, by his touch. It is hard to explain, but it all felt right. How could anything that feels so right be wrong?

The next day, another wonderful thing happened. Mischa told the boss I was ready to learn to use the sewing machine. We spent all morning together while he showed me how to operate, thread, peddle, and place my hands around the needle so I wouldn't get injured. When he put his hands on mine to get them in the proper position, Diary, I looked all serious, but inside, I was a bubbling brook of joy.

Dear Diary,

I'm worried. I told Cousin Sadie about Mischa. She scared me by saying, "Fannie, be careful. I heard about Mischa at the hat factory where I work. He is trying to help get better pay and conditions for all workers. That is admirable, but he's also known as a freethinker. He doesn't believe in marriage. Fannie, do you want to have a baby and not be married? You would shock your family, and frankly, you would shock Itzhak and me. There is a rumor that his religious father is upset with him for shaving his beard and even cutting off his *payes*. Fannie don't get me wrong; he is working hard to get us better pay and make the factories safer. Too many of us workers get hurt on the job. He has a pleasant manner, but I think your family wouldn't understand if you got romantic with him."

Diary, what should I do? I think I am losing sight of why I came to America. It was to take care of my family, not to fall in love. But Mischa brings me the most happiness I've known since I left home to go to Budapest. He seems so caring. And yet Sadie, I know, wants the best for me. What should I do?

I'm writing all this on a copy of the *The Jewish Daily Forward*, and here is *A Bintel Brief* again. I wonder if they answer questions about love? Here is a letter.

"Dear Bintel Brief,

I am a greenhorn. I came to New York to marry my husband. It was all arranged from Bialystok, and we married one week after I arrived. He is a nice enough man, a hard worker, but I pine every day for home. He is getting angry with my tears and my indifference to him. I want to go home so much. He is threatening me with a get. Please advise me."

"Dear Homesick from Bialystok,

What you are going through is long a part of our culture. You took on a lot, leaving your home and family, coming to New York, and getting married immediately. However, you must be patient and give yourself time to make this big change. Have faith that time will heal your home-sickness. Also, you say he is a nice enough man. That means you can hope that love will grow, but it will only grow with time, patience, and faith in our great traditions that have carried us through adversity for thousands of years."

That was a fair response, and kind, too. Maybe I should write my letter.

Dear *Bintel Brief*,

I am a greenhorn, around 16 years old. I came to America by myself. I met a boy who I think I love. My friend who knows him warns me he is a freethinker and does not believe in marriage. He shaved his beard, but his father, with whom he lives, is a religious man. I was raised to be religious; I know the prayers and am expected someday to be a good wife to a religious man. I am not interested in getting married soon, but I love this boy who brings me happiness no matter what he does or doesn't believe. Also, as a working woman in a factory, it is hard to keep all the religious laws in America the way my mother does in Galicia. I think I am slowly becoming American.

Bintel Brief, please write and advise me. My cousin thinks this boy is dangerous, yet I feel happy and safe with him. I don't want to lose the joy I feel for the first time in a long while.

Dear Very Young Miss Greenhorn,

Feeling love is a blessing, even when we make an unwise choice of whom to love. It is not clear that this young man who makes you feel safe is wrong for you. You will need some time to tell. You mention his father is a religious man. Father and son live together, which suggests that while they may disagree, they remain bonded as a family.

Even if you can't always keep our religious laws, there is also a blessing in preserving our culture and traditions. I suggest you offer to make a sabbath dinner for this father and son. You should include all the prayers and rituals of a sacred family gathering. Father and son, each in his way, will value your offering. With the father present, you will be well chaperoned. Such an event will give you more of a sense of the respect that lives between father and son despite their different philosophies.

The next day when I saw Mischa after work, I said to him, "Mischa, did you and your family enjoy shabes in Russia?" His eyes lit up.

"Oh yes, Fannie. I miss that special weekly family time. My mother—may her memory be for a blessing—was a wonderful cook, and even though I'm not religious like my parents, I loved it when my mother lit the candles and said the shabes prayers. I always felt a beautiful mystery as she covered her eyes and gracefully circled her beautiful slender hands over the flame."

The door was open, so I said, "Mischa, I would love to make a shabes dinner for you and your father. It would be a good way for me to meet him, and we can all enjoy shabes together."

"Fannie, what a good idea. Give me a list of what you want to cook. I'll shop for it."

I decided I'd bake a challah, then a *cholent* with lots of barley and vegetables, so there would be plenty for the sabbath day when no one can cook. We will end the meal with apples and honey. This will be a wonderful feast for Mischa, his Tateh, and me too; the best meal since leaving Bolekhiv. I gave Mischa the shopping list, and he added some wine to it.

When I told Sadie my plan, she agreed to let me prepare the meal in her kitchen. I baked two challahs and gave one to Sadie and Itzhak. I also prepared enough cholent for them. Mischa will come by, and we'll bring the food to his place. I always dress modestly but was careful to look very clean with my dark clothes well-ironed.

Mischa's father is older than I expected. He's a little bent over, with large, sad brown eyes. His voice is deep and quiet. He bowed a little when Mischa introduced us. I did the same.

Father and son live in one tiny room with a kitchen at one end, a table, three chairs, and one bed. I guess Mischa and his father share the bed.

I put the cholent on the back of the stove to warm. It smelled spicy and delicious, like Mama's cholent. The sun had not yet set, so while our shabes meal warmed, Mischa suggested we go for a walk. There was a gentle breeze, and the streets were not crowded because families began gathering indoors to prepare for shabes.

While we walked, Mischa said he wanted to tell me a dream he has for the future. "Right now, Fannie, I'm committed to helping factory workers get decent pay and improving the safety of the factories."

"Misha, I admire you so much. You are a man of honor to care so much for us workers and our safety. I see people hurting themselves on the machines every day."

"That's right, it's terrible, and they are not getting paid enough. You should also know, Fannie, I have an even bigger dream for some time in the future. I want to go to Palestine, our homeland. I want to be part of the Zionist movement to build a Jewish state where our people can thrive and be safe."

Diary, I didn't know what to think. Was Mischa telling me this to prepare me for his leaving America? Does he have any vision of a future that includes me? How can I be thinking about a boy in America who wants to go to Palestine someday, while my family is suffering, and my dear Esther may die? How can I even imagine going to Palestine when I have a family who is not safe in Europe and is counting on me to at least help them, if not bring them here? Diary, despite all these difficult things to think about at once, I am overjoyed to be with Mischa.

We went back to Mischa's apartment. His father sat at the head of the table. I lit the sabbath candles and said the prayers. Then all together, we said the blessings over the bread and wine. When I looked up, both men had tears flowing down their faces, and seeing them, I too felt my tears flow. Mischa's Tateh said, as if it were a prayer, "Someday, may we all be home again."

Mischa responded, "When we are with the people we love, we are at home, wherever that may be." I wonder if Mischa envisioned Palestine when he said that.

We finished the meal, and Mischa's Tateh said a prayer to end the meal. Then he began to sing A *Shabesdike Zemerl* and many other Yiddish songs. Mischa leaped up to get his fiddle and started playing. I did not sing at first, but then Mischa's Tateh motioned for me to join in. It felt wonderful. We sang, clapped, and stamped our feet. I want to believe the people on the floor below heard the joy in our music and joined in.

Soon Mischa's Tateh, still sitting in his chair, leaned on the table and began dozing off. Mischa motioned to me to come to the kitchen sink, where he filled a basin with soapy water, so we could wash the dishes. I brought over the dishes. He took them, put them aside, then clasped my two hands in his and pulled both our hands under the sudsy water. He whispered into my ear, "Since that day I touched your hands while teaching you to use the sewing machine, I longed to touch your hands again. Here we are!"

His father stirred. We froze. Then we heard loud, rhythmic breathing. We relaxed.

Diary, it is hard to describe what it was like touching Mischa's hands under the soapy water. We were so together, yet alone at the same time. The warm, sudsy water soothed and thrilled me at once. Our four hands together were exploring beautiful landscapes. Our palms, fingers, thumbs, knuckles, and even nails, caressing, sliding, entwining delicately under the soapy foam. It was only touching hands, yet it was like shooting stars, hearing birds, and waterfalls. I pictured my mountains at home and the smell of warm rain. We slid our four hands over and under each other, both in plain view yet hidden by the warm blanket of suds. My eyes were closed. I opened them briefly and, looking up at Mischa, saw his eyes were closed, his head tilted upward. We were both rocking gently from side to side as if we were dancing together. I don't know how long we were like this, but we both heard his father stir. And we each reached for a dish to wash. Diary, I never felt like this before.

Mischa walked with me back to Itzhak and Sadie's apartment. We parted, but our eyes lingered on each other. I looked back as I went up the steps and opened the outer door. Mischa still stood there. I waved, and he circled his arms as if in a hug.

But then, as I entered the apartment and started to get ready for bed, I realized, to my horror, that I didn't have Esther's blue shawl tucked into the waist of my skirt. In a panic, I ran back toward Mischa's apartment, and by the time I was almost there, I saw him running toward me with the shawl in his hand. Diary, I was so relieved. It must have come loose from my waistband.

Mischa knows about Esther, and he knows the shawl is my tie to her. Oh Esther, how could I have forgotten your shawl? I always check it when

I come and go anywhere! I promise you, Esther, I will never lose it again. Our *Bubbe* wore her shroud wrapped around her waist until her death. Esther, your shawl will be my shroud.

Chapter 6: The Angel of Death

A few days later

Dear Diary,

I received a letter from Rivka:

"Dear Fannie,

Mama does not know I'm writing to you. She wants to protect you from our troubles because she thinks you have enough of your own as you struggle to send us money and settle in a strange place.

You need to know that Esther is very weak. She is now bedridden and barely responds to us."

Diary, I got this far in the letter and couldn't go on. I've never felt so much pain. I couldn't catch my breath, and I curled up on the floor. Sadie came rushing to me. I handed her the letter. She held me while I sobbed like I've never sobbed before. How can I be on this earth without Esther? I've never existed without Esther. We were together from the moment we were first made. I wanted only one thing at that moment, to be home again.

Sadie rocked me there on the floor for a long time. I couldn't bring myself to read the rest. Sadie asked if I wanted her to read it to me. "Yes," I said. I showed her where I stopped reading.

"Fannie, the money you send is so helpful to us. We are managing well enough, except for all our grief about Esther. The doctor comes daily, but it is clear he has no remedy for her. He tells us to sing to her and tell her stories, which we all do, even little Jacob and Kayla. Our Esther is never alone, day or night. When the day is warm, we bring her outside. Fannie, I know that telling you about all the love and care our family is giving to Esther cannot comfort you. I suspect by the time you receive this letter; our beloved Esther will have passed. Her memory will always be for a blessing.

We have heard from Tateh. He has tuberculosis and is in a sanitorium in the mountains. A nurse who cares for him wrote to tell us. She says in her letter that he is weak, and his recovery will take a long time, but he is getting good care. We haven't written to him about Esther's grave illness. I write to you because I know how close you and Esther have always been, and I didn't think it right to keep it from you. Sometime soon, I will let Mama know I wrote to you.

Fannie, please take some comfort in how your earnings in America help our family. With Tateh unable to provide, you are doing a great mitzvah for the family you love and who love you.

Rivka"

Sadie and I stayed on the floor with her arms around me for a long time. Eventually, she got up and made me a glass of tea with extra sugar. I slept a little. Whenever I drifted off, I soon snapped awake, remembering Esther, and sobbed until exhaustion sucked me into another brief bit of sleep.

In the morning, I walked to Hannah's house to tell her about Esther. I gave her a note for the boss telling him I was sitting *shiva* for my twin sister and would be back to work in a week. I also wrote a separate note for her to give to Mischa.

During the week, I sometimes left the apartment. I walked through the city, wrapped in Esther's blue shawl. I walked streets I knew, and walked streets that were new and strange.

How can I be on this earth without you, Esther? I dream of you every night. In my dream, I cry out, "Esther, you're here, you're well!" You answer, your voice, matter of fact, "Of course, I'm here, I'm your twin. We've never been in the world without each other."

Then I wake, and you die all over again. I walk and walk, my mind is full of you, full of our memories, full of our home together, full of my love for you, and though I think of only you and walk with only you, you cast no shadow. Your shadow was seized in a moment in Bolekhiv. It happened day or night when I was unaware. How could I not know? How can I be alive and you not? I'm a tree in winter stripped bare. I'm a broken shell. I'm an empty house. I'm you. The wind keens through my bones chanting *Kaddish*. We were made at the same moment. How can I exist without you? Yet here I am. Only my pain tells me I'm still alive. I hope, my beloved Esther, you are now without the pain of your failing heart and struggling breath and without the pain of knowing death was coming soon.

The week went on. Time moved slowly. Itzhak and Sadie welcomed Mischa and his father to sit with us. They brought almond cake and wine. Of course, Hannah came too, and brought a pot of soup and some apples. They wanted to know about Esther, my family, and our life in Bolekhiv.

Coming to America is so hard. Yet as I sat in mourning for Esther, I was also aware of being encircled by new, dear friends: Mischa, his father, Hannah, Sadie, and Itzhak. All these people bring me warmth and comfort in this harsh world. And yet, I wish I was in Bolekhiv.

I picture my family and try to imagine their shiva for Esther. They're all seated on low benches the rabbi brought in. Little Jacob is on Mama's lap and Kayla is on Rivka's. Kayla is asking question after question. My brothers Aber, Yehuda, and Lazar are talking to the rabbi and planning a *minyan* for the evening prayers.

I was as young as Jacob when my *Zeyde* died, and about Kayla's age when Bubbe died. I remember that. There were ten of us in my family before I left home. Now there are only seven: no Tateh, no Esther ever again, and no me. Will I ever see any of them again? How many shivas will I sit for my family? How many shivas will be so far away from the people I love?

At the end of this long week, I got up, as usual, to go to the factory. The only reason I was able to go was knowing I'd meet Hannah on the way and see Mischa. When I approached the building, I saw a group of people outside surrounding Mischa. They were talking about the poor working conditions, the dangers of the machines, fire escapes in poor repair, and low wages, especially for the women. Mischa was all fired up. He asked if people were willing to strike again. They had gotten a few improvements after the last strike.

Soon the starting bell rang, and the workers went to their stations. Mischa turned, saw me, and ran over. He saw how sad I looked. He is so sensitive. Tears sprang from his eyes for me. Maybe for himself, too. His mother died, but he doesn't often speak of her. We planned to meet right at the same spot after work.

When we met again, the weather was getting cold. I, of course, had Esther's shawl wound around my neck. We stood together shivering, and Mischa wrapped his arms around me while I cried onto his chest. Once I could stop, he said, "Fannie, I want to spend the rest of my life with you. I still have a mission here in America to help the workers get fair treatment, but eventually, I want to go to Palestine with my father and soon bring the rest of my family there. Fannie, please come with me. We will join our Jewish sisters and brothers there to build our own nation. We will create lush farmland out of the desert and even create a new language, modern Hebrew. We will take Hebrew names and stand safe and tall as Jews. You don't have to answer me now, but I want you to know my dearest wishes."

Oh, Diary, I'm in a torrent of feelings. It is getting clearer; Palestine for Mischa is more than a dream. He really has a plan.

This is the worst time of my life. I am now and forever without my twin, and yet a man who loves me and who I love wants to spend the rest of his life with me, a man offering home. But Palestine! I can't work and send money to my family from Palestine. I can't even let myself think about Palestine. I know Mischa said this intending to comfort me, and I believe he means it. But I wish he didn't mention Palestine again.

Then he said he hoped I would share shabes with him and his father every Friday. I could not help but smile when he added, "And after, we will wash the dishes."

Chapter 7: The Serpent Shall Eat Dust

November 1910

Diary, I have not written to you for months now. The days have been cold and gray. I continue working in the shirtwaist factory, usually making around four dollars a week because I now have the skills to operate a sewing machine. I send home two dollars every week, give Sadie a dollar for rent, and keep a dollar. Now that I have a little money, and you, Diary, are so important to me, I bought a student notebook to write to you. I carefully rolled up the pages of *The Jewish Daily Forward* I used to write on, made the thin paper into a sturdy roll, and tucked it into my rucksack for safekeeping.

Sadie insists on providing me with food, and every Friday, Mischa buys groceries for our shabes. For no reason, he brought me a gift, a shirtwaist of my own to wear for sabbath and when we go dancing at the settlement house. We do both the traditional dances and together have learned some of the American social dances. When I wear the shirtwaist, I don't feel like such a greenhorn, but I can't imagine ever feeling American.

When I visit Mischa, his father always greets me warmly. He calls me "Fannie," but sometimes calls me *shaina maidel.*

Hannah continues to be a good friend. She loves Saul, but her family in Lviv insists she marry the son of her father's former business partner.

The son lives in Brooklyn and is doing well as a garment cutter. She is thinking of eloping with Saul and moving to Chicago.

I think Mischa realizes he upset me with his wish to go to Palestine. He has not mentioned it again. He is busy with the workers, trying to organize them to demand safer workplaces and better pay. Mischa is passionate about everything: his organizing, his fiddle playing, and I have to say, about me too. Every day he tells me he loves me, and his father loves me, and that being with me always makes him happy. I love him and his Tateh too, and yes, I'm happy when I'm with Mischa alone or at our shabes table. Yet I feel an undertow of sadness when I think of Esther gone and the suffering of my family.

Roving gangs of men and boys continues to attack Jews in Galicia. My family and I both know I'll never earn enough to bring them to America. The best I can do is send them a little money to help them with the necessities.

I haven't mentioned Feter Oscar in a while. Sometimes I see him on the street with his filthy baby carriage full of old clothes. He never runs after me because he fears someone will steal his stinking baby carriage. But if he sees me, he shakes his fist and yells, "You owe me money. I better get that money, or you'll be sorry."

Last week at the factory, it was payday. All the workers were leaving their shifts. I had four dollars tied up in my handkerchief and tucked into the waist of my skirt. As I walked out, I saw Feter Oscar. He didn't have his baby carriage. He pushed through the crowd of workers, glaring at me with hatred. I tried to get away, but there was no place to run. He ran toward me and backed me against a wall. Screaming in my face, his spit spraying out of his mouth, he yelled, "I know you have money. Give it to me, or I'll report you to the police for stealing and whoring."

Suddenly Mischa appeared. He got between me and Feter Oscar and motioned me to run away. I got about 20 feet away, and I saw Mischa yelling at Feter Oscar, who was now backed against the wall. Mischa was staring him down, and Feter was cowering; then he ran away like a rat.

Mischa came over to me and said, "He won't bother you again."

"What did you say to him?" I asked.

"I told him I know he steals those old clothes he tries to sell. He steals them from the public baths while people are bathing; he steals them off clotheslines and from the *shvitz*. He even steals women's clothes from the *mikveh*."

"I can't believe you told him he steals from the mikveh! What did he say?"

Mischa, imitating Feter cowering and whimpering, said, "Oh no, no, no, I never steal clothes from the mikveh. I never go near the mikveh."

"Then I yelled back at him, 'I know you don't go; you send your wife to steal.' Then I told him if he ever bothered you again, I'd go to the police and report him. He skittered away like a cockroach."

"Mischa, how did you know he steals all those clothes?" Mischa laughed.

"I don't know, I just guessed. I threw in the mikveh just to get his goat. I guess I succeeded! He's a crook and an idiot. Just wait until some customer sees their missing clothes in his carriage. If he had any brains, he would tear up those clothes and sell them as rags. Then he would be a ragpicker and a smarter crook."

I didn't know whether to laugh or cry. I was so relieved and loved my clever Mischa all over again.

But later that night, as I was trying to sleep, I suddenly woke up with the thought, "Feter Oscar is a thief and so am I." I never fell back to sleep. But by morning I told myself to shake it off and move on.

Chapter 8: Out of the Burning Bush

Friday, March 24, 1911

Dear Diary,

Months have passed since I wrote to you. Letters from Mama and Rivka try to reassure me they are doing well. But Rivka writes that Mama is crushed by Esther's death. I'm crushed too, and yet, I still feel the force of life in me. The love I feel for Mischa must explain it. Esther was the one I loved more than anyone else. If I didn't have Mischa, where would my love go? Again and again, Mischa tells me he loves me, and I tell him I love him. I always say it after he does. Why do I always wait for him to say it first?

Every Friday night, we have shabes. Saturday, after sundown, we walk the dark streets of New York, always beyond the Lower East Side. On Sundays, we meet again and explore New York. We often sit on a bench in Washington Square and sometimes go as far uptown as Central Park. There, we like to believe we are in the countryside again. We both miss the trees and plants of home, the farm animals, the wide sky, and open land.

Mischa and I have a game. Sometimes we pretend we are in Russia near his old village and sometimes we make believe we are near Bolekhiv. And so, we introduce each other to our old homes.

One Sunday, Mischa brought a Hebrew Bible. He turned to "The Song of Songs" and read a few verses in Hebrew, then translated them into Yiddish so I would understand.

"The Song of Songs" is his favorite part of the Torah. He is so loving, and dear, and talented in many ways. Sometimes I feel a little intimidated, maybe not so little.

Another Sunday, we went to Coney Island and visited a fortune teller. She saw marriage and children in our futures, but she did not say we would marry each other. I wanted to ask her if she thought Mischa and I would be together but was afraid of the answer. I worried it would be "No," but if it was "Yes," I feared it would be in Palestine. I'd be abandoning my family. I can't work and earn in Palestine the way I earn here. In every letter Rivka writes, she tells me how she, Mama, and all the family are so grateful I send them what little money I can.

I miss my family and grieve for Esther, yet I have to say right now, life here is better for me than it was. The city's filth is still awful, but maybe I'm used to it. Feter Oscar pays no attention to me anymore. I guess Mischa really scared him away. I don't know what's ahead. If I let myself think too much about it, I get scared. Now I have Mischa, Sadie, Itzhak, and Hannah; in some ways, Mischa's father is a Tateh to me. This is a blessing, but at the same time, my own Tateh is still very sick.

A few days later

Rivka writes:

"Dear Fannie,

Tateh's tuberculosis is making him weaker all the time. Our family is not allowed to visit, even if we could make the trip up the mountain. The mountain air isn't curing his lungs."

So, while things here in America are better, I can't keep out the thought that I probably won't see my Tateh again, and maybe neither will my family. Will I ever again see anyone I left behind?

Diary, you hear most of what I have on my mind, while my letters home leave out what I know would worry them. When they write to me, they may be doing the same. I'm at the mercy of my guesses about them, as I suppose they are about me. As happy as Mischa makes me feel, I can't imagine ever not feeling homesick.

Sunday, March 26, 1911

Dear Diary,

I'm in shock. Yesterday afternoon, a fire broke out at the shirtwaist factory. If I worked on the 9th floor, I would likely be dead.

It was horrible. We finished work for the day and were getting ready to leave the 8th floor when I heard screams from the other side of the room, then smelled smoke. Flames rose to the ceiling and quickly burned through the floor above. We all ran to the door. The place is so big, and there are so many of us. The girls in front banged on the door. It was locked. It's always locked. They banged and banged. No one came. Then all of us ran to the window to a fire escape. I was at the back of the crowd. The girls ahead of me climbed onto the fire escape and

65

started running down when another crowd from the floors above also came down.

Soon we heard a deafening sound of breaking metal and screams, screams, screams. The fire escape collapsed under the weight of so many people. Those still on the 8th floor were trapped. Smoke filled the space. Suddenly I felt a hand grasp mine. It was Mischa. He shouted for everyone to follow him to the elevator. He had been out of the building, saw the flames, and ran in. He tried the stairs, but they were filled with thick smoke, so he brought one elevator up to the 8th floor. We crammed in. The elevator can only hold eight of us at a time. We ran out on the ground floor, but Mischa kept going up and bringing people down again and again. I waited outside for him.

The nightmare on the ground was unbearable. The fire ladders didn't reach past the 6th floor. Women on the 9th floor were trapped. As the blaze grew, many jumped out of the widows with their clothes on fire, instead of perishing in flames.

I'll never forget the sound of bodies hitting the pavement. I'll never forget the blood and the tangle of limbs. I'll never forget the smell of burning flesh. I'll never forget the sirens and the screams. I'll never forget my fear as I waited in the crowd, searching the doorways for Mischa and Hannah to come out. Hannah came out first, not from the building, but from around the corner. It was a miracle. She works on the 9th floor, but just before closing time, her boss asked her to bring a tally of the day's finished shirtwaists to the 10th floor, where the owners and bookkeepers have their offices.

As the fire reached the 10th floor, the top floor of the factory, students at New York University, a taller building only feet away, stretched ladders from their windows to the factory roof. Some students came to help. They pulled people out of the tenth-floor factory windows onto the roof. They could then climb up the ladders into the University building and get down to the bottom floor and out onto the street. That is how Hannah got out. I ran to her, and we held each other. She sobbed and sobbed. So many of the women she worked with were horribly injured or dead. She could not believe how lucky she was to have been on the 10th floor at that moment.

Finally, finally, Mischa came out. He made many trips up and down with the elevator, bringing people out of the 8th floor. He couldn't go higher because flames started coming down the elevator shaft. He was covered with sweat and soot. His hands were burned, and he coughed from the smoke. That elevator I hate and Mischa, who I love, saved many lives.

Afterwards, Mischa and I walked back to his apartment. His Tateh, terrified, was waiting outside for Mischa to return. When he saw us, he ran toward us, blessing G-d for saving us both and embracing us together.

We went upstairs, and I helped Mischa clean his poor burnt hands. I made poultices from cold tea and clean rags from a neighbor, then wrapped each hand. I had seen Mama do this often when she burned her hands cooking. Mischa said the tea soothed the pain. Then I made him some hot tea with sugar and added some *schnapps* that his father brought out. Mischa could not hold the glass, so I spooned the warm tea to his lips. When he had the last spoonful, he cleared his throat, closed his eyes, and rested his head on my shoulder.

I left and returned to Pike Street. Itzhak and Sadie were outside waiting for me. They had heard I was all right. We slowly walked up the stairs, sat at the table, and said the blessing. Sadie had cooked a warm and comforting potato *kugel*.

Before going to sleep, I wrote to Mama and my sisters and brothers, saying, if they hear about the fire, they should know I escaped it and am safe. Also, I would soon figure out how to find work.

Chapter 9: A Time for Every Purpose

Dear Diary,

On Monday morning, I went with Sadie to see if I could get a job at her hat factory. I hoped to earn the same pay as at the shirtwaist factory because I could use a sewing machine. The supervisor told me they didn't need sewing machine operators, but I could be a baster. I stitch the parts of the hat together by hand with long, even stitches. Then the sewing machine operators can quickly sew everything into place.

I was so busy working and trying to gain this new skill that it was not until Thursday that I looked around and felt sick. I work on the 9th floor. There are two floors above.

Diary, this is what happened. First, I saw dozens of cardboard boxes lying around as well as all the scraps of felt. The supervisors all smoke. They suspect the fire started at the shirtwaist factory when someone threw a lighted cigarette into a bin with paper and fabric scraps. The room here is as big as the 8th floor at the shirtwaist factory. Suddenly, I saw the tangled and burned bodies again. Again, I smelled the burned flesh and felt like I was choking on the smoke. I couldn't breathe. My heart was pounding. Everything went dark.

When I opened my eyes. I was on the floor, lying on my back. One of the older women held my head and tried to get me to take a sip of water. "Are you pregnant?" she asked.

"No," I said, and slowly got up. I was dizzy but could get back to my seat, where I tried to work. I couldn't. My hands were shaking. The supervisor came by and yelled because I was not keeping up with the work. Finally, the end-of-the-day bell rang. I met Sadie downstairs. She looked at me and gasped,

"You're so pale, Fannie. What happened?"

"I don't know. Suddenly, I thought I was back at the shirtwaist factory in the fire. I guess I fainted."

"Oh, Fannie, you can't return to this job." She held my arm all the way home. We sat drinking tea, and after a while, she said, "Fannie, I think I'm pregnant."

I looked closely at her. She was shining. I grabbed both her hands and all the horrors of the past week slipped away. She continued,

"It's only the second month, so I'm still holding my breath, but I have all the signs." Then she said, "I have an idea. When the baby comes, if you will do piecework at home, you can take care of the baby while I continue to work at the factory. I need to keep working at the factory, because Itzhak earns no money. He is dedicated to studying Torah, hoping to become a rabbi."

Diary, my heart was beating hard again, but this time, it was out of joy for Sadie. Then I stopped and thought, how will I earn enough to send money home and cover my expenses only doing piece work at home? Before I could figure out how to bring this up, Sadie said, "Since you will be such an important part of our family now, I will not take any rent money from you. It will help if you can put in some money for food. I think you will still be able to send your family something." Sadie had an idea for piecework, too. "The coat factory, the same one you sewed buttons for, sends out a lot of piecework. The pay is best for sewing machine operators. I have a sewing machine you can use. When my aunt in Brooklyn became a midwife, she gave it to me."

I hugged Sadie. What a good person she is and what a relief to not have to work inside a factory! And I get to take care of her baby!

April 1911

Diary, life has changed since the fire. Sadie's plan is working. I'm staying in the apartment and sewing the lining into men's coats. Itzhak is here all day, studying and praying, unless he goes out to the shul. He says nothing to me all day, but sometimes when I look up, I think I see his head jerk down at his books. Was he looking at me? He never says a word to me. Itzhak has always been quiet, even when we all have a meal together. He says the blessing, of course, and I hear him saying his prayers and reading scripture, but I don't think I've ever exchanged words with him, except for greetings and good night. Recently, when I'm in the room, he is more than quiet. He is silent.

Dear Diary,

Sadie seems to be holding onto her pregnancy. I'm so happy for her. She is tired after work, so I've taken over cooking supper.

Another big and difficult change is that I don't see Mischa often. We saw each other every day when we both worked at the shirtwaist factory. He tried to get another factory job but had trouble, because the bosses see him as a labor agitator. He has always tried to get better pay and safe workplaces for all workers, but after the fire, he is even more passionate about it. He talks about the workers and workers' rights all the time. He says, labor organizing, not religion, is his calling. He reads a writer named Karl Marx, who he says guides his convictions. Sometimes he reads Karl Marx out loud to me. I try to pay attention.

Does he still see Palestine in his future? He has not spoken about it. And for all my reasons, I don't ask.

He helped his father mend shoes for a short time, but soon picked up jobs here and there doing construction. He is still affectionate and sweet, but he is very preoccupied. When I don't have time with him, I feel homesick and lost without my Esther. Did Mischa become my Esther?

We always have shabes with his Tateh, and we are together on Sunday, but only in the evenings. Sundays are when he has his organizing meetings.

One Sunday evening, we went to the Yiddish Theater on 2nd Avenue, and guess who is a stagehand now? Hannah! I hadn't seen Hannah since the fire. After the play, the three of us met and talked. She wants so much to act with the theater company. They told her if she started as a stagehand, she would get to know the theater and eventually try out for parts, maybe first as an understudy. I don't know how she is earning any money.

I received a letter from Rivka:

"Dear Fannie,

Little Jacob is not only walking; he is running, and Kayla wants to go to school. Yehuda wants to leave school and learn carpentry to work with Aber. There has been no word about Tateh. Mama continues to be very sad. I try to keep our family going. I do the cooking now, and tend to the garden and the animals. Thank goodness the cow and chickens are healthy, and the vegetables are growing well. We have plenty of potatoes and cabbage. I made a barrel of sauerkraut, and the potatoes are all stored safely in the cellar, so we are set as far as food goes

I often find Mama sitting alone and staring out the window at nothing. There is no joy left in her. She speaks rarely, but when she does, she says she wants to find a way to send the older boys to America. She fears they will be taken into the military. She says as Jews, they will be sent to the most dangerous positions.

She is heartbroken about Esther and suspects Tateh will never leave the sanitorium.

While she appreciates every bit of money you send, she misses you terribly. She says you were the one who could always raise her spirits.

Love,

Your sister, Rivka"

I wonder if Rivka will ever get married. The family needs her so much now.

Tuesday, May 2, 1911

Dear Diary,

Mischa helped the workers at one of the factories to strike. He was between construction jobs, so he joined the strike, and some thugs tried to interfere. A fight broke out. Mischa was pummeled but not really hurt, but then he and a group of others were arrested. Mischa spent a day and a night in jail! He's ok. He's back to his construction work and continues to organize the workers. Now he attends meetings at night as well as all day on Sundays.

Several Days Later

Diary, something horrible happened. Last Tuesday night, I heard a knock on the apartment door. I opened it and was surprised to see Mischa. He was pale and shaking, then broke into tears. We held each other, while he sobbed.

He calmed a little, saying, "Fannie, get your shawl and come sit on the stoop; I need to talk to you."

We went downstairs and sat very close to each other. He took my hand in both of his and again wept.

"Mischa, Mischa, what is it?"

He caught his breath. "Yesterday, my Tateh was coming home from shul late in the day. He took a shortcut through an alley. Halfway down the alley, he heard running behind him. He turned, and three thugs knocked him to the ground. One guy punched him hard in the face, breaking his nose, then grabbed his yarmulke and pushed it onto his face so he couldn't breathe. Another guy kicked him, breaking some ribs. They left him on the ground, writhing in pain."

I gasped and started to cry. Mischa tried to comfort me. He knows my Tateh was beaten up and robbed at the salt mine. I got some control, and Mischa went on.

"Finally, someone came through the alley and ran for the police. An ambulance came and took Tateh to the hospital. He's in a lot of pain. He keeps saying, 'Is this why we came all the way to America? We could've stayed in Russia to get beaten. I don't want to bring over the family to get beaten.' Fannie, he is in so much pain and angrier than I've ever seen him." Mischa then got very quiet and looked away. He soon turned toward me with so much anguish in his face,

"Fannie, I think the attack on Tateh was because of me, because I organized the strike. I know, yes, I know, religious men with beards and yarmulkes get attacked even in America. He shouldn't have gone into the alley, but these are criminals hired by the bosses to go after the labor agitators. They stop at nothing. They go after the families too, even children and old people."

Diary, what I must tell you next is so painful, I'm not sure I can write about it. Maybe I can write about it as though I'm telling Hannah, who I hardly ever see anymore, or maybe I could imagine telling it to Esther. But I need to write it too. I need to write it and tell it as though I'm talking to someone my age who I completely trust and can comfort me. Sadie is wonderful, but I can't tell her because it is about Mischa. As much as she has come to like and respect Mischa, as you know, she is suspicious of what she calls his "freethinking."

I must go sit on the stoop to write. If I'm alone, I'll cry so hard I won't be able to stop. With people around, I'll have more control.

Dear Diary, or maybe Dear Esther or Dear Hannah,

I will try to continue and tell what Mischa said.

He paused; he took a deep breath. He looked away, then turned back to me. My stomach knotted up. I could barely breathe. I knew what was coming.

"Fannie," Mischa sobbed again. "Evil wins this time. I can't let my Tateh be at such a terrible risk. Fannie, my Tateh, and I must go to

Palestine now. I talked to him about it. He agrees. Fannie, I'm afraid they'll try to kill him; they could have killed him this time. They'll do anything to try to stop me from organizing the workers." Mischa gulped. He grabbed my shoulders, looking deeply into my eyes. "Fannie, please, please, please, will you come with us? I can buy your passage."

It was here. The question I knew would come now came like a boulder, first slowly rolling down a mountain, speeding up, now blasting into me. It arrived, that big question, "Fannie, will you come with us to Palestine?"

I couldn't breathe until a huge sob burst out of me. Mischa gave me time to catch my breath. "Fannie, I know this is not the way we imagined things but try to think about it and let me know in a day or two. Try to get some sleep tonight; I will too. I'm going to buy the tickets in a few days. A ship leaves in ten days for Marseille and from Marseille to Palestine, but I must get the tickets soon."

We held each other for a while. Was this the last time? It was dark and the streets were empty. Reluctantly, we let go of each other. Mischa returned to his apartment, and I came upstairs. Sadie and Itzhak were asleep in their room. I lay on the sofa, not bothering to get undressed, but just wrapped Esther's shawl tightly around me.

I cried and cried as I saw so much before my eyes. I'm still crying. Mischa and his Tateh will leave. They must leave. Esther died. My Tateh is dying, Mama is despondent, and my family is struggling and depends on the money I send them. I may never see any of them ever again. Maybe Mischa can eventually bring his family to Palestine, but he can't bring all of mine, too. If I go with Mischa, I abandon my family in Bolekhiv. If Mischa doesn't go, he abandons his Tateh. Suddenly, I know in a way I haven't let myself know, Mischa is the center of my life, my safe harbor, my anchor. Because of him, I go on even after losing my Esther and probably soon losing my Tateh. Mischa loves me, and I love him. My love for him is new but also feels like family love, especially when we are together with his Tateh. If I don't go to Palestine with Mischa, I abandon him, he abandons me, and I'm alone. If I go to Palestine, I abandon all my family in Bolekhiv. I will never have the money to bring them to America or Palestine. I never imagined how hard all this could be. My heart is more than broken; it is torn apart.

May 3, 1911

I finally slept a little, and when I woke, I wrote to *A Bintel Brief* explaining what happened and my dilemma. I hope I receive an answer soon.

May 5,1911

The response appeared in the paper today.

"Dear Young Woman with a very wounded heart,

You are forced to make this very painful decision so quickly because of the cruelty that sadly exists in the world. There is no correct answer except the one you think you can live with right now. Inevitably, you will have times when you regret the decision you make. Life will be a harsh desert for a while. I hope before too long; you find some oasis, some soothing spring, some peace.
Bintel Brief"

Chapter 10: Honor Thy Father and Thy Mother

D ear Diary,

I can't sleep. I have little hope of ever seeing my family again. But I can help by sending money. Will I ever see Mischa again after he leaves? I don't know. I don't dare hope. Mischa is not as poor as we are. He doesn't need me to be in America. My family needs me to be here. I must try to sleep. I need strength more than ever before.

I fell asleep briefly and had a dream:

Suddenly people are throwing money at me. Who are they? Just what I need is coming at me. I try to pick it up from the street. As I reach for it, the wind blows it away. I chase after it. They keep throwing more and more and more. I slip, falling on all this money. Money covers me. It's in my mouth, in my eyes. There's so much of it–piles and piles on top of me–heavy, pressing me to the ground. I can't move. It buries me. I can't breathe. I can't scream.

I woke up coughing and choking. It felt so real. Money, money, money! I'm weighed down with so much obligation to send money to my family! What about loving Mischa? What about my life? I don't even feel grown up yet. Why did Mama send me to America? Why not one of the older boys or Rivka? If I bring Mama so much joy, why did she get rid of me? I don't want to think this. I hate myself for thinking this. If I lose Mischa, I can't be angry with Mama. Who else do I have?

If I had stayed in Bolekhiv, I would not have met Mischa. Mama, who wants so much for me to get married, would have arranged a marriage with someone I didn't know, let alone love. I've never been so angry in my life, not even in Budapest or at Feter Oscar. I'm stuffed with anger about money and being the one expected to make it and send it home. If Esther had been well, would Mama have sent us away together? I wish I was the sickly one and died; then, I would not have to hate myself for this terrible, selfish anger. I want Mischa. Without Mischa, I have no life. I just earn money. That's all I'm good for. If I never met Mischa, I'd be better off. I wouldn't feel so much pain. Oh Mischa, sweet free-thinking man, I wish we never met. Love is too painful, too dangerous.

The Next Evening

Diary, my heart hurts. It's so heavy I can't carry it. It's Friday and I could barely walk to Mischa's place. Will it be our last shabes together?

When I arrived, Mischa was already sitting on his stoop, and I sat next to him. Mischa looked different to me. He almost looked stern, no smile, his body stiff. He didn't take my hand but looked straight ahead, saying nothing. I knew he was waiting for me to speak. I ached all over. My mouth was dry. I could barely get the words out. When the words came, they felt like thick dry paper.

"Mischa, if I go to Palestine with you and your Tateh, I will abandon my family who need me here to send money to them. They depend on it."

Mischa was silent for a long time. At first his words came out like a written speech, matter of fact, almost cold. "Fannie, I tried to prepare myself for what I suspected you'd say, and you just said it. You knew I was thinking of going to Palestine eventually, but not so soon. I had work to do with the workers here. I would not go now if my Tateh hadn't been beaten in the street, probably because of me. You're staying in America to be a good daughter to your Mama. I'm going to Palestine now to be a good son to my Tateh."

With his head in his hands, he was silent for many minutes. I put my hand on his back. He shook it off. Then he loudly moaned, "I have stab wounds all over my body!"

Suddenly a wail like I never heard came out of him. His body trembled and shook with deep gasping sobs. He let me put my arms around his wracking body. He was flying apart. My tears wet his shirt. People passed us. They looked, then moved on quickly.

We sat for a long time. Neither of us wanted to move. Moving meant we were coming closer to a moment when we would tear apart from each other. But eventually we did move and walked upstairs to his apartment where his Tateh was waiting. Looking at us, his Tateh knew the decision. He sighed, embracing us both. Then Mischa's Tateh gently took my head in his hands and said a blessing over me. Then did the same with Mischa.

Except for the shabes prayers, we ate in silence. We didn't wash the dishes. Mischa walked with me back to Pike Street. He will write, he said, as soon as he knows where he and his Tateh will live. Then just before we parted, he said, "The ship leaves next Sunday at Noon. Fannie, please come to the pier. Get there early and find a place as close to the ship as possible. I want to be able to see you as we sail."

This will be so painful for us both, but I agreed to go.

Sunday

Diary, I arrived very early at the pier as the passengers slowly boarded. Finally, I saw Mischa and his Tateh on the first deck. They signaled they also saw me. People on the ship threw streamers to people on the pier who grab them. Mischa motioned, he was going to throw a streamer to me, but it looked different from the paper streamers everyone else was throwing. He aimed it, and it came right to my hand. I grabbed it. It was a narrow red ribbon, weighted at the end. Something was wrapped in a bit of paper. I opened the paper. It was a message and wrapped inside was a heavy gold ring. The message read, "I sought and found whom my soul loves." "You are beautiful, my love, as lovely as Jerusalem." [2]

The ship's whistle blew. Smoke rose from the stack. Four tugboats slowly hauled the ship from the dock. The ship sailed. Mischa let go of his end of the ribbon. I gathered it in and held it to my heart.

---

2 From "The Song of Songs."

Chapter 11: The Desert

Diary, I stayed at the pier until the ship was out of sight. Mischa is now surrounded by water, and I'm in the desert. It is a hot, even though it is only May. I walk home through unshaded streets. What shall I make of Mischa's note and the ring? It can't be a promise. Is it a wish for us to be bound to each other although many thousands of miles apart and no plan for a future? Is this gift manna in the desert, or is it a mirage? Love is so dangerous. Loss is love's shadow.

Mischa transformed me from a child into a woman. After the experiences in Budapest and with Feter Oscar, desire was frightening. I never wanted it. I hid from it. But with Mischa, he was my beloved. My desire was toward him and his toward me. He protected me. He protected the workers. He is protecting his Tateh. I could not protect him, or my Tateh, or Esther. I know I brought Mischa joy. Except for our last meeting, he glowed every time we met. But I couldn't keep him safe. I can send money home to the family I love, but I can't keep them safe.

When I arrived back at Pike Street. Sadie was out with Esther. Itzhak was *davening* over his Torah. I curled up on the sofa, and although the weather was hot, I wrapped myself in Esther's shawl and Sadie's quilt.

The door to the apartment flies open. Mischa stands in the door frame.

"Mischa, you're back!"

"Of course, I'm back. Tateh is on his way to Palestine. I'm here for you." We
embrace.

I snapped awake. My arms embraced only Sadie's quilt, and Mischa left again. This is cruel. Will Mischa keep haunting my dreams only to disappear again across the sea?

Again, as I did when Esther died, I go out onto the streets and walk. I walk all the paths Mischa, and I took on Sundays and before our shabes dinners. I'm numb. In one hand, I grip Mischa's ring and the circle of red ribbon. As always, Esther's shawl is tucked into the waist of my skirt. I will sew a tiny bag of black velvet with a drawstring to store the ring and red ribbon and then wear it around my neck. My body is weighted with my loves, my losses, and my shroud. Is the happiest time of my life over?

August 1911

Days and days pass, then weeks and almost three months—there is no word from Mischa, and I'm shocked to find myself angry. The ring and ribbon are a burden. Why is he tying me to him when we are unlikely ever to find our way to each other? He is clever and sweet, but it is always his way. He decided when the women at the factory were ready to use the machines. He chose to spend Sundays organizing the workers, and he decided to go to Palestine. Is this what Sadie understood and was trying to warn me about? Am I a puppet dancing to his tune, held up by a red ribbon? He threw the ribbon and ring, hooking me like a fish. But he let go. Mama let me go. Why? Did she want to get rid of me, one less mouth to feed? I want to think she sent me because she had faith in my cleverness. The younger ones were too young to go. The older ones were already working, except for Yehuda. Why didn't she send him, or the two of us? She wouldn't get rid of him. He's her favorite. He was named for her brother, who died as a child.

Esther was too frail and could never earn money. She could barely take care of the little ones. She thought of herself as a drain on the family. I hate to think of her as a drain because she was sick. Mama thought I was strong and independent for my age. Then along came Mischa, and I let myself lean on him and take care of me. I wasn't at all strong when I was with him. He always led the way, and I loved it, and I loved him. Do I still love him? It scares me to think I'm so angry that I don't love him. But he gets everything he wants. He wanted Palestine all along. He says he wants me and loves me, so why doesn't he write? I can't just wait. I have no other way to reach him except to wait for his letters. If I never met Mischa, I wouldn't feel such pain.

I'm not going to suddenly become rich and have the money to bring my family and myself to Palestine, so I must wait for what Mischa can do, if anything. He will not earn money in Palestine. He'll be a farmer. Yet he's trying to hold on to me with a red ribbon, a ring, and some poetry. All I can do is hope and yearn for him. I don't think he has any idea how angry I can be. Only since coming to America, when I stole the dress from Feter Oscar, did I begin to realize how furious I am with Mama, with America, and now with Mischa.

Diary, I was taking one of my long walks toward uptown, and who did I meet? Hannah. I thought she might have moved. I hadn't seen her in the neighborhood since the fire. She looked different. I barely recognized her when she called to me. She looked beautiful, elegantly dressed like a wealthy American with an expensive shirtwaist. Her hair was swept up, and she wore a hat with a big brim and a large feather plume. She carried a yellow hatbox. She had been shopping. Something about her appearance changed, not only her clothes. Her face is fuller, and I think she might have gained some weight. It is becoming. She looked womanly.

We had a quick conversation. I told her I was doing piecework, and still living with Sadie and Itzhak. What she said puzzled me.

"Fannie, I'm doing well. I live in one of those nice buildings on Washington Square, and I don't have to work at a regular job. I met a man who is taking good care of me." Then she took a deep breath, straightened up, and looked as though she was ready to move on to wherever she was going.

"Hannah," I said, before she could take off, "What happened at the Yiddish Theater? Are you getting the chance to act?"

She looked at me a moment and said quickly, "That didn't work out. I am better off now. I must run."

She looked beautiful and healthy, but also troubled.

September 1911

Finally, a letter from Mischa.

"Dearest Fannie,

We changed ships at Marseille and sailed to Jaffa, where members of the kibbutz Degania greeted us. We arrived at the kibbutz several hours later. The ship was hard on Tateh, but the journey from the ship to the kibbutz was the hardest. He felt dizzy in the desert heat and fainted a couple of times. Our hosts were kind. They brought him water, which revived him briefly.

We have now been on the kibbutz for several months. Our fellow kibbutzniks are welcoming, high-spirited, and fervently dedicated to making Palestine a homeland for all Jews throughout the world who face antisemitism.

We all study Hebrew and intend to modernize it so that it becomes the official shared language of Jews. They gave me a new Hebrew name,

Micah. Everyone but Tateh calls me Micah. Tateh's new name is Natan. So, I am Micah ben Natan. I like the sound of it. I hope you do too.

The woman's Hebrew name I love is Shira, meaning 'song.' I think of you here in Palestine taking the name Shira. It reminds me of when we recited 'The Song of Songs' to each other."

Diary, the letter goes on, but I had to stop reading further at this point. I was so overwhelmed with so many feelings at once. I was swept back to the time Mischa and I felt so entwined and in love. We loved loving each other. And now he is thousands of miles away, with no guarantee we'll ever meet again. I'm filled with yearning for him. It hurts. He pulls me toward him and ties me to him. The only thing that helps is to be angry about his big dreams for himself. He imagines me in his dreams. I already have a beautiful Hebrew name. I live in his imagination, but what about me, flesh-and-blood me? How can we love each other and never be together? My life, my duty to my family doesn't match his plan, so he left me.

Here is the rest of the letter.

"Tateh and I live with other single men in a dormitory. Everyone in the kibbutz eats together in a big dining shed. Our food comes from what we produce from the farm. In this way, it reminds me of home in Russia. Members do the cooking, the farming, cleaning, caring for animals, anything that is needed to sustain our livelihood. We are with each other 24 hours a day. There is great equality here. No one owns more than anyone else. We do not use money because we all do the work we can do and are free to take what we need to live.

The farm is beautiful, a lush green oasis in the middle of this dry land. I am assigned to farm every day. Tateh still repairs shoes, but he also milks the cows, something he did every morning as a boy in Russia.

But I must tell you, Fannie, I'm also surprised by what I find here in Palestine. There is plenty of sandy desert, but there are also cultivated farms created by the Arabs. Arabs have rented land from the Ottomans for generations and created their own farms. They, too, have been turning the desert green long before Jews returned to Palestine after thousands of years in exile.

Sephardic Jews from around the Mediterranean came to Palestine long before we Russian and Eastern European Jews arrived. They are often more urban, running businesses. So, there are the Arabs who have been in this part of the world for thousands of years. There are the Ottomans who made Palestine a part of the Ottoman Empire and claimed ownership of the land, as well as the Sephardim mostly running businesses. These three groups got along, more or less. But with the arrival of Jews from Russia and Eastern Europe, there is new tension.

I will try to explain. Some newly arriving Jews buy land from the Ottomans, including the land already rented and farmed by the Arabs, thus forcing the Arabs off the farms they have cultivated and lived on. It is no surprise that the Arabs feel hostile toward the Jews and sometimes go on raids at night, attacking the kibbutzim. An armed Jewish guard, called Hashomer, was created to protect the kibbutzim at night. There have been confrontations here at Degania.

Also, The Sephardim, who are well off, look down on the poorer Ashkenazi Jews, whom they view as intruders and disrupters of the peace.

Fannie, I guess what I'm trying to tell you is while Tateh and I are escaping American hatred of us, we are finding hatred here in what I had hoped was a safe and welcoming haven. I wish I did not have to tell you this, but I must be honest with you. I have too much respect for you to paint an untrue picture.

Tateh and I have written to our family in Russia. They are ready to leave, but now they think of going to Shanghai, Canada, or South

America rather than Palestine. This could mean that Tateh and I will be on the move again.

I struggle against becoming cynical, but maybe there is no place of peace for us. Despite confronting all this sad truth about hatred in our world, there is also great beauty in love, music, nature, and poetry like 'The Song of Songs.' I love the spirit of the kibbutz. I play my fiddle, and we compose new songs and dances. Fannie, you would love this part of life here.

I look forward to going to bed each night, not only because I'm tired from working in the sun on the farm all day but because I can count on being with you in my dreams. I hope you also dream of me.

I send you all my love,

Your Mischa/Micah

P.S. Here is my address. Kibbutz Degania, via Jaffa, Palestine. The mail goes first to Jaffa, and we must pick it up and bring it here, so it takes a long time."

I don't doubt my dreamer, Mischa/Micah. I live in his dreams, but can I live in his world beyond his dreams? I don't know the answer. How should I respond to his letter? What can I say? Can I allow myself a tiny bit of hope that we'll be together? He's in my dreams, too. He comes back. And like it is with Esther, he says, "Of course, I'm back!" I wake, and he and she are gone again.

I wrote back to Mischa right away.

Dear Mischa,

Here is the news from America.

Sadie's pregnancy goes well. As you know, I'll continue to do piece-work at home and take care of the baby while she returns to work in the factory. We're very excited. She has longed to be a mother for so long. I look forward to caring for the baby, and Sadie seems glad to have me do it, but I know that her heart will break a little every morning when she leaves for the factory. She wishes she could do piece work and stay at home. But Itzhak is extremely religious and scholarly, hoping to be a rabbi someday. Now he earns nothing. I'm often so distressed about how so many decisions we must make have to do with money.

Mischa, or should I call you Micah, I also dream of you most nights. I love seeing you, even in a dream, but when I wake, I miss you like I did at the pier when your ship left, taking you thousands of miles away and my heart with it, stretching it to the breaking point. I carry your red ribbon with the ring, and the words from "The Song of Songs," in a small velvet bag that I wear around my neck.

I'm frightened about the tensions you describe in Palestine, especially the night raids on your kibbutz. Please, please be very careful. You usually step up when there is a chance to be a hero like you did at the fire and with the workers and when you confronted Feter Oscar. I love and admire your courage, but I'm also frightened by it. Mischa, before I met you, I could not imagine loving anyone as much as I loved my twin sister, Esther. You and Esther are entwined in my soul.

Love,

Fannie

Oh Diary, I surprised myself with the letter I just wrote, especially the last sentence. I didn't want to speak that truth to myself, but there it is. Why didn't he mention anything about the red ribbon and the ring?

END OF PART I

PART II

Chapter 12: Shroud

December 1911

A Letter from Rivka:

"Dear Fannie,

I am so sad to tell you our Tateh died. We received a letter from the sanatorium. It feels like a surprise, even though it isn't. We are all grieving. Even little Jacob fusses as though he feels the sadness of the rest of us.

We are troubled because we can't bury Tateh in our cemetery. The sanitorium will bury him in a nearby graveyard. I asked if it could be a Jewish cemetery but haven't heard back. The Rabbi came, and the neighbors too. We talked about what a smart and trusted person Tateh was. That is why he had the job as a paymaster. I couldn't help but think if he had stayed working in the mine, he might be alive today. But maybe not because of the tuberculosis. Although he might have died at home without going through that horrible beating first. We all sat shiva for seven days. May his memory be for a blessing.

Mama doesn't weep like the rest of us. She acts resigned and is unusually quiet. This began soon after Esther's death. She is now bent over and ages more every day. I gave her a cane because I feared she might fall. One night I was helping her to bed. I noticed she now wears a shroud around her waist like our Bubbe.

I am so sorry, Fannie, to trouble you with such sad news. Also, I hear from Lviv there is growing unrest. I don't understand, but it involves the Austrian and the Serbian people and who will rule in this part of the world. The Serbians hate our Franz Joseph, who has been good to the Jews.

If there is war and the older boys are taken by the military, I fear Mama will give up what's left of her will to live.

I miss you, Fannie, especially the comfort your presence would bring, but as I say in each letter I send you, please know how much you are helping our family. We are managing because of your help.

The whole family sends their love to you,

Rivka"

Diary, I'm numb. I can't bear to take on more sadness. Is this how life is for me? Am I destined to lose everyone I love? I loved Tateh. Sometimes he whispered in my ear, "You are my *Abigail.*" I wonder, would he have sent me to America if he was at home instead of in the sanitorium?

Numbness is all I dare feel now. The one exception is I ache reading Rivka's description of Mama growing old and now wearing her shroud, as I am, with Esther's shawl. I fear I am growing old too.

I folded Rivka's letter, tucking it into the quilt I use at night, then returned to my piecework of sewing linings into coats. I'm glad for this repetitive work, the sound of the sewing machine, and the demand that I concentrate on doing it right. I worked until my eyes burned. Looking up, I caught Itzhak looking at me, then immediately, he went back to davening over his Torah.

Chapter 13: Who Will Look After Me?

January 1912

Diary, I haven't written in a while. I move through my days, trying not to think about anything except work, tasks, and helping Sadie. She stopped working at the factory a month ago. For now, she will do piecework at home until she returns to the factory, soon after her baby is born.

Weekends are dreary now. That's when Mischa and I were together and took our long walks. Last Sunday, I walked to Washington Square Park, where Hannah said she now lives in one of the fancy buildings nearby. I was lonely and hoped I might see Hannah there. I sat on a bench and watched families enjoying their day off while I looked out for Hannah. I'm glad I waited. After awhile, she walked out of one of the well-kept brownstones. I called to her and crossed the street to catch up to her. She turned toward me. We hugged each other. I was startled. I realized she was pregnant, as pregnant as Sadie.

After we hugged and stepped back, I saw Hannah looking flustered. I missed her and didn't want her to run off again. So, I said, "Hannah, can we sit and talk? It's been so long since we spent time together." She seemed hesitant at first but then agreed and we sat on a nearby bench. I kept talking, hoping to keep her from walking off.

"You were good to me when I had nowhere to live and needed work. You helped me, and because of you, I met Mischa."

She seemed willing to stay. She asked, "Are you still with Mischa?" I told her about Mischa's labor organizing, the attack on his father, their decision to go to Palestine, and my decision not to go. I didn't tell her about the ring. She saw how sad I was, and she caressed my hair. We were silent for a while then Hannah burst into tears.

"Fannie, as you can plainly see, I'm pregnant. I didn't want to get pregnant, but here it is. I'm with a man who takes care of me, so I'm not poor anymore, but he's married. He demands I place the baby in the foundling home as soon as it is born. I don't want to give up this baby. Once I felt him move, he became mine completely. I'm sure he is a boy. I want him. He will be my family in this strange, lonely country. This man says if I keep the baby, he won't support me. He'll get rid of me."

Hannah sobbed, hiding her face in her hands. I put my arm around her, and she cried even harder. Once she was calm again, she asked, "Do I shock you, Fannie? I let myself get into this mess because I desperately didn't want to be poor anymore. Do you think I'm bad?"

I didn't know what to think about Hannah's plight, but it felt right to be close to her. I said, "Hannah, life here in America is much harder than we ever dreamed. Whatever we must face, we'll face it as friends. Please, let's be friends and help each other. Maybe we can start by meeting here at the park every Sunday." Hannah wiped her eyes and nodded her head. She took my hands in both of hers and kissed them.

"I should go," she said. We stood, hugged again, and parted.

The Following Sunday

Hannah and I met again at the park. As she began talking, I heard her voice shake and she wrung her hands.

"Fannie, I must be honest with you. You may not want to be friends when you hear what I tell you. If so, let's find out now before we get closer. This man, who supports me, pays for my apartment, clothes, and expenses, and gave me money to send to my family. He said he loved me and thought I was talented. He claimed he had connections to the theater and would help me get started. I let myself become dependent on him, and once I needed him and had no other way to live except what he provided, he told me he works with a woman who runs a fancy brothel, and I was to become a prostitute. He threatened me. If I tried to run away, he'd throw me out in the street and report me to the police. He prepared me to be a high price prostitute with a specialty of helping young Jewish men who are engaged to be married. I'm trained to know how to please a man and to teach these young men how to please their wives. Once I started to work in the brothel, this man, his name is Mendl, but he calls himself Jack, withdrew all his support. I earn a small part of what the customer pays the brothel."

She stopped here and asked, "Fannie, I don't know if you want to hear more."

"Yes, Hannah. I want to know what you're going through."

"The woman who runs the brothel showed me the various ways a woman enjoys sex. She believes this work is a *mitzvah* for young married couples. They will look forward to having sex and bear many children. I'm also trained to dress well, learn English, speak without a Yiddish accent, order in a restaurant, and shop for clothes. Fannie, I was weak. I wanted the glamor of being an actress, and I closed my ears to the lies Jack told me. So, this is the kind of actress I let myself become!" Hannah sobbed again. "So many things didn't work out. Saul got involved with someone else and left me. I wanted to work in the Yiddish Theater, but it was clear I would never get more than an occasional small part. And then Jack came along. He attends amateur plays and dances to see if any of the women actors and dancers might become prostitutes. At first, I thought he was being nice. I didn't know he was married. I didn't know he was grooming me to be a harlot. Fannie, I trapped myself. What I'm doing is illegal, and if caught, they could deport me. If I try to leave, he will report me to immigration. I hate being in America, but I hear it is worse to be back in Lviv. If I went back, and they found out what I did here, which they would, I'd face the consequences there. So, I trapped myself."

She continued. "And this pregnancy is a trap too. The only reason Jack keeps me on, is I earn him and the brothel a lot of money. Once I deliver this baby, he expects me to give it away and get right back to work. He thinks I should be grateful he didn't throw me out when I began to show. If I keep the baby, I become a poor greenhorn again, this time with a bad reputation. Fannie, this is my horrible plight. If you want nothing to do with me, I understand. Please, if that is so, leave right now."

Hannah's sobs shook her whole body. When she was able to speak again, she said, "I can't believe I told you all this. I never thought I would ever tell anyone. It all came exploding out of me."

Diary, I wasn't shocked by what Hannah told me because of what happened to me in Budapest. But with luck, I managed to escape, and she didn't. I was more upset by Hannah's intense pain. In her place, I'd want to die. I'm in a lot of pain now because I lost people so dear to me. I'm lonely and guilty of stealing the dress. But I'm not trapped, except maybe in poverty. I don't like my life, but I guess I'm managing somehow.

"Hannah, I don't want to run away from you. We met on the boat. We're trying to find our way in this harsh country. Both of us are lonely.

You've already helped me. I don't know how I can help you, but I know I want to try, and I want to be friends and see you as much as I can."

"Oh, Fannie, thank you. I was so afraid you'd never want to see me again. I need a friend so badly. I earn a good amount of money even though it is only a small part of what the men pay. I was able to send enough for my family to leave Lviv. I sent them to Montreal, Canada, instead of America. I'm too ashamed for them to see what I've become. Maybe someday I can visit them. At least they're safe and not horribly poor."

Hannah and I parted with a plan to meet every Sunday. It feels good to be with her again. It will help me not miss Mischa so much. especially on Sundays.

As I walked home, I felt uneasy, but I couldn't say why. It was something more than Hannah's pain. I never heard of young men visiting prostitutes for marriage training. But what do I know? My world was mostly Esther and Mama.

That Night

I am lying on Sadie's sofa. A huge, black cloud covers my body; I try to push it away, flailing my arms. Then another comes, and another and another. I sit straight up, breathless.

Diary, what was that! Oh no, no, no. I don't want to remember. Forget about it. It's over.

Chapter 14: Mother of Nations

A Few Weeks Later

Diary, Sadie's baby, is coming soon. I'm as excited as she is. Her aunt in Brooklyn, Tante Malkah, is a midwife and will help to deliver the baby. Sadie asked me to help, too. She said, "You need this. It will help you know what to expect when you have your babies." Will I ever have babies? Will they be with Mischa?

I never helped Mama; Rivka did. I wish I had some experience delivering a baby. It scares me. I remember Mama screaming in pain, but as soon as the baby was born, she was all smiles, and that's when Tateh and the kids were allowed in the room. At home, the midwife was a woman from our shtetl who delivered all of us. Twice, the babies didn't survive; once before Yehuda and again before Kayla was born. I don't remember it. It would be terrible for Sadie if her baby died.

Sadie is busy making plans for her delivery and preparing what the baby will need. She will nurse until she is almost ready to go back to the factory.

The next time I saw Hannah at the park, I asked about her delivery plans.

"Jack wants me to deliver the baby at the new maternity ward at Bellevue Hospital. He thinks it's safer. He doesn't care about the baby but wants me to stay healthy because he makes a lot of money from me. He doesn't care except for what I bring in for him."

It startled me to hear such a hard-hearted attitude. Hannah must have seen my surprise because she quickly added, "Fannie, please understand; it's in my best interest too. I need to stay healthy for this work. I earn much more than working at the factory. My family is safe in Canada only because Jack decided he could use me."

I tried not to show how sad I found all of this. Hannah was trapped by Jack, trapped by the work she was forced into, trapped by her need for money, trapped in America. Was Hannah now resigned to this way of life?

Then, remembering how much distress Hannah felt when she told me Jack expected her to put the baby in the Foundling Home, I asked, "Is Jack still insisting you give up the baby?"

Hannah looked all around to be sure no one sitting close to us could hear. "I have a plan, Fannie. I pray it will work out. You must pledge this will be a secret between us."

"Of course, it will."

"I have an Italian friend from the shirtwaist factory. She is one of the few on the 9th floor who survived the fire. She made it down the fire escape before it collapsed. She knows a widow with four kids. This widow, Carmella, also Italian, earns money taking in babies who can't be with their mother. She charges plenty, but I can manage it. I can visit whenever I want, and I'll be able to nurse my baby. My friend explained the situation to Carmella, who doesn't speak much English. Jack can never find out about it. If he knew, he'd surely put me out on the street. Someday, if I ever escape this trap I made, I'll be able to take my baby and maybe join my family in Canada, although I'm not sure they'll have me, given what I have become. But if this works, I can keep my baby, and I can't tell you how happy this makes me." We hugged and parted.

Yet again, money makes a big difference in how life works out. Hannah's plan is a mix of sad and good; my head is spinning. Hannah doesn't have to give up her baby because she has money, but how she makes the money threatens her chance of keeping her baby. My life could have been like hers. I try so hard to forget about the time in Budapest. Someday, maybe I'll tell her my secret about Budapest.

Also, it makes me think of Mischa's new life in Palestine. He's on the kibbutz because someone could buy the land, and he could afford the passage. Yet on the kibbutz, people seem to go about their lives without money.

Sadie asked me to help her plan how to care for her baby after she returns to work. She asked friends at her factory how they managed to nurse their babies and continue working. Some can call upon sisters or cousins to help, but some hire wetnurses. They find them mostly by asking friends. I had seen personal ads in the *Forvertz* requesting or offering wetnursing. Sadie asked me to help her find someone and hoped it wouldn't cost too much.

I wonder if I could ask Hannah to nurse Sadie's baby and her own. I could bring Sadie's baby to her. Is it too much to ask of Hannah? I could see Hannah every day, several times a day. If Hannah agrees, I can tell Sadie I found a healthy woman I knew at the shirtwaist factory, which is true. I could also say she cannot have her baby with her, which is also true. It is not all the truth. I'm helping Sadie, but should I tell her the woman is Hannah? Sadie would ask a lot of questions. Hannah pledged me to secrecy. I can't do that. Hannah is my only friend, I feel close to Sadie, but she is more like a helpful married, older sister, than a friend my age. I'll find out if Hannah is willing, and then I'll decide.

The following Sunday, Hannah and I met again. I was nervous but told myself it was important Sadie's baby do well and be nursed by a healthy woman.

Hannah looked like she could deliver any minute, and so does Sadie. I jumped in, explaining to Hannah about Sadie's situation.

"Fannie, can I really nurse two babies?"

"I have an easy answer. I'm a twin, and our mother nursed both of us. There are other twins in my mother's family. They were always both nursed by the same woman. Sadie can pay a little."

"Oh, Fannie, no, I would never take money to help Sadie and her baby. Does that sound strange coming from me? It would be a mitzvah and let me feel my life was worth something. But Sadie can never know it's me. Only you, my friend from the 9th floor, and Carmella can know I'm keeping my baby," I threw my arms around Hannah.

"Hannah, I've always known you are a good person. I promise to keep our secret."

Hannah wept, and so did I. Why is it so hard to be a young woman alone in this world, this bitter world? But at this moment, my heart bubbled with joy to be close to Hannah again and to know I would see a lot of her. I missed her so much, especially after Mischa and his Tateh left.

Chapter 15: Birth Day

February 15, 1912

Diary, I have so much to tell you. Sadie had her baby today. Her water broke, and she had contractions throughout the night. I could hear her moaning in bed. Itzhak went to Brooklyn to get the midwife, Sadie's Tante Malkah, and her apprentice niece, Zelda. They arrived at dawn. Also, a neighbor came in.

Tante Malkah examined Sadie and said, "This should be soon." Sadie had collected a lot of copies of the *Forvertz* from the neighborhood, and Tante Malkah laid them out on the bed and on the floor.

Itzhak stood in the doorway. He shook all over, muttering his prayers. Tante Malkah yelled, "Itzhak, go wait in the hall." To us, she said, "Fannie, Zelda, I want each of you to take one of Sadie's legs. When I say push, you hold her legs apart and push her knees toward her belly. When I say 'stop!' you let her rest until I say 'push!' again." Motioning to the neighbor, she said, "You stand at Sadie's side. I want you to keep talking to her and wipe the sweat off her face."

Sadie screamed in pain. Tante Malkah yelled, "Push Sadie, push, push, push!" Again and again, Sadie screamed, and Tante Malkah yelled "Push!" This went on and on. I could see Sadie was getting exhausted and Tante Malkah began to look worried. Then I heard Tante Malkah mumble under her breath, "*Oy, veh iz mir*, this baby doesn't want to leave its Mama."

She shouted to me, "Fannie, set up a kitchen chair, and put more *Forverts* on the floor." Then, her voice suddenly calm, she said to Sadie, "Sadie, we're going to get you in another position so this sweet baby will want to come into the world and into your arms." She helped Sadie to stand up and Zelda and I, on each side of Sadie, held her as we walked with her to the chair.

Pointing to Zelda, Tante Malkah instructed, "Zelda, straddle the chair and push yourself all the way back. Sadie is going to sit between your legs and push her back against you. You are going to hold her tightly under her arms and around her chest as she pushes. Fannie, you, and your neighbor are going to hold her legs."

Tante Malkah knelt between Sadie'slegs holding open a small blanket. As soon as Sadie pushed, Zelda didn't have the strength to hold onto her. Tante Malkah told her to get up. Zelda slid out from behind Sadie.

Then I heard Tante Malkah call out to Itzhak, "Itzhak, get yourself in here. You have work to do. We need your man strength. You're going to have to help your wife."

Looking stunned, Itzhak came in from the hall. "Now sit far back in the chair and straddle your legs on both sides, like you're riding a horse. You've ridden a horse, haven't you?" Itzhak nodded. "You're going to hold Sadie up and not let her fall off the horse."

When she spoke to Sadie, she was tender. "Sadie darling, now I want you to sit between Itzhak's legs. He's going to help you." Zelda and I settled Sadie down between Itzhak's legs.

"Now Itzhak, wrap your arms around Sadie, under her armpits and around her chest." Itzhak froze, so Tante Malkah lifted each of Itzhak's stiff arms and placed them around Sadie. He was thinner than Zelda, so Sadie also had more room on the chair.

"Now, Itzhak," said Tante Malkah; she was stern again. "Sadie is in labor. She's counting on you to hold her with all your strength while she puts all her strength into delivering this child of yours."

We were ready. Zelda and I went back to holding Sadie's legs. Tante Malkah took her position again. As the contractions came, Tante Malkah again yelled, "Push, push, push, push!" Sadie moaned, then screamed with pain. Tante Malkah kept saying, "Good, Sadie, very good. The baby is coming now. At last. It won't be long now. I see the top of its head."

The baby's entire head emerged, face down at first, then turned toward me. There was a lot of very dark hair. I don't know why, but I began to cry and could feel my heart beating faster and faster. I yelled, "Sadie, your baby is here! I see the face!"

Soon the top of the body was out, then the whole body. There was a big gush of blood. Then it stopped. Tante Malkah cradled the baby in the blanket. The baby was white, almost bluish, arms and legs pulled in, a little ghost figure. I was frightened, but Tante Malkah was calm. She held the baby's feet up and let the head be toward the floor.

"Come on baby!" cooed Tante Malkah. Then with a little rubber syringe, she sucked stuff out of the baby's nose and mouth. The baby stretched, then cried out a good loud cry, and turned pink. "Good!" yelled Tante Malkah. She cleaned its body with a cloth, and gently smoothed salt over the baby's skin. Next, Tante Malkah took a piece of cotton string, tied, and knotted it around the umbilical cord close to the baby's body. Then, leaving a small space, she took another piece of string, again wrapped it around the cord and knotted it. She handed me a pair of scissors, telling me, "Fannie, you are going to give this baby her freedom." She told me to cut the cord between the two strings. It was tough, like gristle. It took two cuts of the scissors to get through.

Then Tante Malkah yelled, "Sadie, Itzhak, *mazel tov*, you have a perfect daughter."

She handed the baby to Sadie, who placed her against her breasts. Sadie cried and laughed at the same time. "Hello, my little girl!" she cried as she nuzzled the baby's head. "I waited for you for so long!"

"Sadie," said Tante Malkah, "We have one more job to do." Tante Malkah took the baby girl and handed her to the neighbor. "You will get her back very soon Sadie, but I need you to push again." Sadie pushed, and out came a big bloody thing. I gasped. Tante Malkah said, "This is good. This kept the baby safe and fed while she was growing inside Sadie. It's all out now; Sadie will be fine." Then Tante Malkah asked me to make some tea with bread and jam for Sadie.

Tante Malkah helped Sadie into her bed and brought her, her baby. She settled her comfortably and helped her to get started with nursing, even though the baby will soon have a wetnurse. I heard Tante Malkah give Sadie advice about stopping her milk before she returned to the factory. But then came a loud wail from Itzhak, followed by sobs. "What's the matter with him?" asked Tante Malkah.

Sadie said, shrugging, "There's nothing we can do. He wants a son."

"*Meshugana!*" muttered Tante Malkah, slapping her hand on her head and then through the air, dismissing Itzhak's antics.

And then, Diary, I almost can't believe what I heard next. Sadie called to Itzhak, "It's all right, my husband. We will name this strong girl for your mother, Esther. May her memory be for a blessing." Then under her breath, "I hope that will help him."

"Esther!" I gasped.

"Yes," said Sadie, "but remember Fannie, she is named only for Itzhak's mother, which means you can still use the name when you have a daughter." I put my arms around Sadie and baby Esther, and cried like I did when I lost my Esther, my twin sister.

So, here I am in America. I will help care for a new Esther, yet I couldn't care for my Esther at the end of her life.

I'm tired but still excited. Before I sleep, I'll write my family and Mischa about all that happened today.

Later

I finished the letters and slipped under the comforting quilt. As my eyes closed, I suddenly remembered Tante Malkah asking me to give baby Esther her freedom.

It's difficult to describe how I felt after cutting the cord. It's a necessary part of the work of birth, but it was so much more. I think something deep inside my body woke up. I'm not sure, strange, lonely, thrilling? I separated this baby from her mother. I'm separated from my mother and lost my twin. My body is free of my family. But my dreams, memories, and feelings of duty are tightly tied to them. Am I free? If I had felt free, I probably would have gone with Mischa. Hannah isn't free. Will this baby ever be free? How do we become free?

Chapter 16: Milk

Diary, Sadie, and baby Esther are spending a few days recovering. Sadie wraps herself around Esther, nursing her and cooing to her. They both look so peaceful. Sadie enjoys nursing Esther as much as Esther enjoys it. I suspect Sadie is storing up her memories and feelings of this blissful time. I wish she didn't have to stop her milk and go back to the factory.

During these days before I take over Esther's daytime care, I'm getting to know her. When she gets fussy, usually in the late afternoon, if I swaddle her in a small blanket and pace the apartment, she calms down right away. I remember Mama swaddling baby Jacob and walking with him. Kayla, as a baby, didn't like swaddling. She always wanted to kick her feet and wave her arms. Babies seem to know what they want right away.

Today is Sunday, so I left Sadie and Esther alone together and went to meet Hannah for our now regular Sunday visit. As I approached our usual park bench, I was shocked to see Hannah holding a bundle, half hidden under her coat, and sure enough, she was holding her baby. She lifted off part of the soft woolen blanket showing me her beautiful baby boy.

"His name is Daniel."

"When was he born, Hannah?"

"Five days ago, a bit early, but he's doing well."

"Is Jack letting you keep him?" I asked hopefully.

"No, Fannie, he wants him out of the house tomorrow. He refuses to have a *bris*, even with no one else present. Since he believes Daniel is going to the foundling home, Jack thinks it's better they don't know he's Jewish. I don't know if Jack is protective or if it's yet another way to convince himself this baby has nothing to do with him. My heart is breaking, but I'll bring him to Carmella tomorrow. She's a kind woman. The timing is good because she doesn't have another baby with her right now. At least I'll see him every day for as long as I'm nursing him. If Jack finds out I didn't give him up entirely, he will be furious. He can get rough."

I told her about baby Esther, who was born three days ago. Then I slipped my arm through hers. We sat silently for a while. I felt myself heave a huge sigh and said, "We were two kids on that boat coming over, full of hope for ourselves and our families. Look at us now, two sad women weighed down with life."

We planned the times of day and night when Hannah would regularly go to Carmella's house to nurse Daniel, and I would come at the same times so she can also nurse Esther.

"It's a short walk from here, Fannie. Carmella lives close by in the Italian neighborhood, on the other side of Washington Square."

I asked, "What will Jack think when you go out several times a day?"

"I already go out every day to shop for food, to have my hair done, or take a walk. He never comes around at night. I told Jack I would take extra walks to get my figure back. That satisfied him."

Before we parted, Hannah asked, "Fannie, I'm so nervous about leaving Daniel at Carmella's tomorrow. Will you come with me? If you bring Esther, I can nurse them both for the first time."

"I'll be right beside you, Hannah, and I'll bring baby Esther. Sadie returns to the factory soon, so she needs to stop her milk."

We parted, with a plan to meet the next day and go to Carmella's apartment together.

When I told Sadie I found a healthy wetnurse for Esther, a friend from the shirtwaist factory, she was grateful. "What does she charge for being a wetnurse?" she asked.

"My friend won't charge because she wants to do a mitzvah."

"Why would she want to do that, Fannie?"

"I'm not sure, Sadie. I offered her what you could pay. But she said, she didn't think it right to charge for her milk." I wonder what Sadie would think if she knew it was Hannah.

The next day, as planned, Hannah and I met; Hannah carrying Daniel and me carrying baby Esther, wrapped in my Esther's blue shawl. We walked to Carmella's apartment.

Carmella is an ample and kind woman, and despite being a young widow with children, she is lively and energetic. It surprised her to see someone with Hannah. It was hard to explain the situation to Carmella. Among the three of us, no one spoke or understood much English. I can't tell if she understood that Esther is not my baby, but she seemed to understand that Hannah would nurse both babies. She turned to Hannah, acting out, rocking, and holding one baby to one breast and the other baby to the other breast. She put a hand on Hannah's shoulder and, with the other hand, patted her own heart, saying in English, "You good Mama. You help." We all understood.

Hannah brought Daniel to her right breast. I gave her Esther, and Hannah brought Esther to her left breast. Esther had no difficulty with the change. She nursed hungrily. Both babies fell asleep. Then Hannah let me take Esther from her. With an anguished face, she handed the sleeping Daniel to Carmella.

Hannah slowly stood. Her arms were now empty. She slipped one arm through mine. Hannah, Esther, and I slowly made our way back to Washington Square. I watched Hannah heavily walk up her stoop. Esther and I returned to Pike Street, and I placed the sleeping Esther into Sadie's arms.

Chapter 17: Order and Disorder

August 1912

Diary, it's been many months since I last wrote to you. Life is quieter now. Sadie is back working at the hat factory. In the evenings, she arrives home breathless; she must run all the way. She takes Esther into her arms and holds her from the moment she arrives until she must leave the following morning. Esther sleeps through the night. I don't have to bring her to Hannah in the dark anymore. Esther babbles and turns over and tries to sit up. The best moments of my day are when she smiles and squeals while I play with her.

Hannah and I spend time together going to and from Carmella's place. Being with Hannah comforts me. I'm so glad I have this time with her.

The nursing goes well. Hannah has plenty of good milk, and both babies thrive. All that is good, but I feel a heaviness. My family and I exchange letters about our daily lives. In my letters, I leave out the sad news. I suspect they do the same. Except Rivka lets me know Mama is still despondent. This must be terrible for Rivka. She is still a young unmarried woman yet has the full burden of the family.

When I'm not leaving the apartment to bring baby Esther to Hannah, I do piecework for the coat factory and tend to Esther. Also, I've decided, I need to learn English. I find English hard to learn. I look at *The Forverts* and then look for the same story in an American newspaper. Hannah and I try to converse in English. I don't think I'll ever be able to say that ugly *th* sound.

Itzhak sits at the table studying and praying, which is not unusual, but he pays no attention to Esther. I have never seen him even look at her, let alone hold her. I can't imagine my Tateh or Mischa's Tateh having no interest in their own baby, even if they were hoping for a son.

I wrote to Mischa again. Although he told me letters take a long time to arrive, I've heard nothing back from him. Has he forgotten me? What should I make of it? I have a place to live, enough food, the pleasure of watching two babies do well, a good friend with Hannah and a new, older, and caring sister with Sadie...yet I'm still so lonely. I'm around 17, yet I feel much older. I think about how happy and young I felt with Mischa before the fire. That fire and the attack on Mischa's Tateh tore apart my life with Mischa.

Just writing this makes me weep. I realize I not only love Mischa and miss him, but I also love his Tateh. Every shabes, when he put his hands on my head to give me a blessing, it was like he cradled me. Oh, Diary, I must stop. I feel so sad right now.

A Week Later

Diary, something strange is happening with Itzhak. Sometimes when he bends over his Torah and davens, he shakes his body, then with a wild look, sits up and shouts, "Where did you get that baby?" He puts his head in his hands, muttering "Sodom, Gomorrah" and weeps. Sometimes he runs out of the apartment as if he's being chased. He comes back a little calmer. Is he going to the shul? I hear him crying in the room with Sadie at night and listen to her trying to comfort him. But last night, he wasn't only weeping; he was screaming, "It's not mine!

It's not mine, you whore!" It was scary. I don't know how Sadie stays so calm. She keeps trying to soothe him.

Last night was the worst. He was howling like he was in terrible pain. He yelled, "I did nothing. I don't know how she got that baby. I did nothing!" Again, Sadie tried to soothe him, but she couldn't. I heard pounding on the wall. I was frightened for Sadie, so I opened their door. Itzhak was beating his head against the wall, and Sadie was helpless. Finally, Itzhak spun like a dervish and fell to the floor, seeming to faint. Sadie handed me Esther, who was crying. Sadie ran out the door, yelling over her shoulder, "I'm going to get the rabbi."

Itzhak didn't move, but I could see that he was breathing and soon just whimpering. He had a bloody gash on his scalp.

Sadie returned with the rabbi and his helper. They lifted Itzhak onto the bed, and the rabbi said many prayers over him.

I could hear the rabbi telling Sadie that Itzhak had a dybbuk, a tormenting spirit possessing him. Tomorrow the rabbi will return with a minyan to exorcise the spirit. In the meantime, Sadie should gather some candles, a vessel of clean water, a saucer of salt, and some pure oil. These will all help to cleanse the spirit from Itzhak. The rabbi left. I told Sadie I'd gather and put all things the rabbi wanted on the table.

Sadie took a bottle labeled "Carbolic Acid" from the kitchen shelf, along with a jar of honey. With Itzhak's head in her lap, she put some of the carbolic acid on a clean rag and gently cleansed his wound. He moaned softly. When it was clean, she could see the shape of the gash. It was a long gash and it looked painful. She opened the jar of honey and spread a small amount over the wound. Then, she put two fingers into the jar and brought her fingers to Itzhak's lips. He licked her fingers, sighed, and fell asleep.

The Next Day

The rabbi returned with nine men making a minyan. They all put on *tefillin*. Sadie, holding Esther, and I were told to stand outside in the hall. They shut the door. If actual words were spoken, we couldn't hear them. We heard waves of sound, first whispers, rising louder and louder to shouting, then diminishing again to whispers. Sadie said they were trying to call out the evil spirit, releasing it from Itzhak's body.

Suddenly we heard piercing screams. First, it was a man's scream, then a woman's scream. It sounded like Sadie's screams when she was in labor. Next, it was the sobbing of a young child. Soon there were loud sobs in Itzhak's own voice. Finally, the men were silent, but Itzhak continued to cry. Then Esther started to cry. Sadie told me to bring her to the wetnurse. Thank goodness it was almost time to go and meet Hannah anyway.

When I returned, the rabbi and the nine men were gone. The rabbi told Sadie, Itzhak had two dybbuks: a female demon, and an unborn child. He also said it was good Itzhak had the long gash on his head, because the spirits could escape through it.

Sadie was pale and exhausted. She whispered, "If I have more children, I'll never again allow Itzhak in the room until after the baby is born, whatever the circumstances. I'll have an army of women ready to help"

Itzhak slept all day until evening. I had cooked a cabbage soup for all of us, and Sadie brought a bowl to him. I heard Itzhak ask how he got the cut on his head. He remembered nothing.

Chapter 18: The Truth

September 1912

Diary, I betrayed Sadie. Now I'm facing the consequences. I was horribly selfish. I secretly asked Hannah to nurse Esther so I could have time with Hannah every day. I need Hannah's friendship, but it was not fair to Sadie. She is my caring big sister; my Rivka in America, and I hurt her. Here is what happened.

On Sunday afternoon, baby Esther was asleep; Itzhak was at shul, and Sadie had just finished washing diapers when she turned toward me. She looked troubled.

"Fannie, I need to ask you something. Why doesn't Hannah visit us anymore? I thought you were close friends. Do you ever see her?"

My stomach went into a knot. I was dizzy. I'm sure I got pale. Here it was. After more than six months of Hannah secretly nursing Esther, secretly hiding Daniel, and the secret of why she was hiding Daniel, it was all going to come out. What would happen to Hannah and Daniel? I either had to lie to Sadie or betray Hannah. No lie in the world could cover this. Then I realized that all Sadie asked was why Hannah didn't visit. But why did Sadie ask about Hannah? I answered with a partial truth.

"I see Hannah when I go out. The Yiddish theater didn't work out, so she's figuring out what to do. What makes you ask, Sadie?"

"

"Well, Fannie, at the factory, I heard a rumor from my friend, one of the Italian girls, she talked about a woman named Hannah. My Italian friend has an Aunt Carmella, a widow with four kids. Carmella takes care of babies when their mother can't be with them. This Hannah wears beautiful clothes and comes at least three times every day to nurse her baby boy. She comes with a poor woman with a baby girl. Hannah nurses the little girl too. The aunt doesn't know why the poor woman can't nurse her own baby."

Diary, I was dizzy again when I heard this. Sadie went on: "Then my Italian friend, Carmella's niece, told me something horrible. Hannah is a known prostitute."

Now Sadie was upset, very upset. She was shaking, getting red in the face. Her voice got louder and louder. "Fannie, can this be true? Could this possibly be your Hannah, your friend who visited us? Fannie, please don't tell me a prostitute is nursing my baby!"

There it was. Nothing I could say was going to make this all right. I had to tell Sadie the truth, and I had to tell Hannah that people know her secret. She's in big danger if Jack learns she kept Daniel. I took a deep breath.

"Sadie, yes. Hannah is the Hannah you know, and yes, she has a baby boy a few days older than your Esther, and yes, she is nursing both babies. It's hard to say this...." I took a deep breath, "Yes, she is a prostitute. But...."

I tried to go on, but Sadie sprang out of her chair and paced the small room, back and forth, back, and forth, pulling at her hair, then her blouse, breaking the threads, then throwing up her hands, "G-d in Heaven!" she wailed.

Shaking, I went to the stove and made tea with schnapps. Finally, Sadie sat down and sipped it. I thought she had calmed a little, but suddenly she glared at me, her fists clenched, her voice rising to a shout.

"Fannie, I trusted you and helped you so you could keep sending money to your family, so you could work at home and not have to work in a factory. Most importantly, I trusted you to care for my most precious Esther. Behind my back, you bring her to a prostitute to be nursed! How can you do such a thing? You betrayed me and put my treasure in the hands of a prostitute! Oy veh. Oy veh. I can't believe this. I don't want to believe this." She got up again, paced again and making a fist beat her breast. I got in front of her, trying to stop her.

"Sadie beat me, don't beat yourself." She pushed me so hard I fell backward onto the floor. I wasn't hurt but Sadie looked shocked and sat back down.

Sadie put her head in her hands and cried huge sobs. Slowly, she stopped and looked up at me.

"Fannie, I've grown to love you, and now I find out about this. How could you do such a thing to Esther and to me?"

We were quiet for a while. Sadie had turned her back to me. Finally, she turned toward me again, giving me a sad and puzzled look. I said, "Is it all right for me to talk now?"

"Let's hear it," Sadie said coldly.

"Sadie, I've grown to love you, too. You are the first person to help me feel safer in America. You have become a big sister to me, my Rivka....."

Sadie interrupted, shouting, "I know all that! Tell me what I need to know."

"I'm trying to explain about Hannah and me so you can understand it all better. I've just told you that the rumor you heard is true. But there is more to it. I'll start by saying I know what I did is wrong. And you may want me to leave this house and never come back."

"Okay, okay, go on."

"Hannah and I met on the boat coming over. We were two girls, around 16 years old, traveling alone. On the boat, we saw sickness and death. Neither of us knew what was ahead."

"Fannie, get to the point!"

"I'm trying. But I must tell you things you don't know about first, so you can understand how all this came about."

"Okay. Go on." Sadie put her head down on the table, her arms folded over her head. she couldn't bear to look at me.

"From the ship, I went to live with my Tateh's brother, Feter Oscar. I never told you Feter Oscar refused to pay me unless I let him make use of my body. I escaped with nowhere to go and no money. I thought I'd have to beg and sleep on the street. Hannah came to my rescue. She also had run away from her sponsor. She lived with four other girls. It was summer and she said I could sleep on her fire escape. She took a big chance. If her landlord found out, he would have kicked her out. She found a job at the shirtwaist factory and helped me to get a job there too. Thankfully, Mama could write to your Itzhak, and you were both generous to let me live here in this tiny apartment. You've been only kind and good to me, giving me a home here in this hard country. But, Sadie, you're right; I should never have made this plan with Hannah."

Sadie lifted her head and looked at me again. "So why did you arrange this with Hannah behind my back?" Then, screaming, "I want to know why my baby is nursed by a prostitute!" Sadie waited for an answer.

I went on. "Hannah wants to be an actress...."

Sadie interrupted, yelling, "I don't care about Hannah's ambitions. I want to know why you betrayed me."

I broke down and sobbed so hard I thought I'd pass out. Then it all came bursting out. "I've been unbearably lonely since Mischa left, since the fire, since coming to America, since my sister and my Tateh died. Hannah and I met on the boat. She was alone, too. We took care of each other. After the fire, she disappeared. I never heard from her. After Mischa left, we met again on the street. She was pregnant and troubled. I wanted to hold onto her, see her, and be with her. You needed a wetnurse, and Hannah was healthy. I took it as a chance to be with Hannah again. I was selfish and desperate. If I told you the wetnurse was Hannah, and she was a prostitute, you never would have agreed to it."

"Of course not!" Sadie's tone softened a bit. "Hannah seemed like a fine girl. How did she get herself in so much trouble?"

"Sadie, I'll try to explain. She met a man who pretended to be romantic and protective, and she got pregnant. It turns out he was not only married, but his money came from working for a woman who owns a brothel."

Sadie shuddered, then asked, "So why didn't she run away?" I waited a moment.

"Sadie, it's a complicated story." She seemed ready to listen, so I went on. "This man seduces young girls, usually greenhorns, pretends he loves them, sees that they have a place to live, and gives them money to send to their families. Once they depend on him for survival, he tells them he's been preparing them to be prostitutes. He warns them if they try to run away, he'll report them to the police, and they'll be deported and live in shame. If they try to stay in America, they are criminals. He holds them hostage. When Hannah got pregnant and started showing, he told her if she didn't put the baby in the foundling home, he'd kick her out on the street and report her to the police. When she felt her baby move inside her, she knew she could never give up her child. She planned to hide him by bringing him to Carmella, your friend's aunt, where he would live and where she could go to nurse him every day, hoping that maybe someday she would have the strength to take him and escape. I asked Hannah if she was willing to nurse Esther along with her son. Selfishly, it was a way for me to see Hannah every day. I knew she could nurse two because I'm a twin. Hannah was not only willing to nurse Esther, but she was also thrilled she could help you and do a mitzvah. She's ashamed of her life and feels she has sunk so low. So, Sadie, now you know. Should I leave your home now?"

Diary, I was shaking and could feel the sweat trickling from under my arms. I was sure Sadie would put me on the street. I stopped talking, and Sadie was quiet for a long time. Finally, she spoke. Her tone was a matter of fact.

"Of course, Itzhak can never know about this. If he knew, he'd get himself another dybbuk" She was quiet again, and her face became sad. "It pains me to think, because I had to work at the factory, my precious baby suckled at the breast of a prostitute. It also pains me that you arranged all this behind my back."

We heard soft babbling coming from Esther's cot in the bedroom. Sadie rushed to pick up Esther and put her on her lap. She offered Esther a piece of bagel from the table. Esther took it, looked at it, then happily gummed it into mush. Sadie nuzzled her nose into Esther's dark curls. Esther looked up at her mother and squealed. Sadie squealed back. They "talked" back and forth, squealing, oohing and ahhing, imitating each other, and smiling.

"Well, Fannie, we do have a fine, healthy little girl here who is getting ready for diluted canned milk and more solid food."

I felt tears of relief fill my eyes and a fullness in my throat. Sadie gave Esther a tin cup to play with while Esther settled, molding her back against the front of Sadie's body and waving the cup in the air.

Sadie sighed and started to speak again. "I don't know if I can ever really get past this, but I want to try. The most important thing in all of this is Esther. Anyone can see she is thriving, happy and growing. And you, Fannie, have become important to me This is a warmer, more lively home since you moved in. As angry as I am with you, I'd miss you if you left." Sadie paused for a long time. I could see that she was thinking.

"It's not easy to come to America for any of us, but when I hear your story Fannie, and hear about Hannah, I realize I had so much more help than the two of you. First, I didn't come alone; I came with my older cousin Zelda, who you met when Tante Malkah delivered Esther. Like you, Zelda and I were sent to America to send money home and hopefully get them out of Poland. Tante Malkah was already here. She came after her husband died. and lived with a relative who was a midwife. That's who taught Tante Malkah the trade. Tante Malkah does well. She doesn't charge relatives, but she is a respected midwife and gets a lot of work. She sent for Zelda and me. Right away she arranged my marriage to Itzhak. I don't know why she rushed into that. Zelda is learning to be a midwife. Although things haven't always gone well, I was never in the danger you and Hannah faced." She paused again, her brow furrowing, "Tell me, what is Hannah going to do now that this rumor, this true rumor, is going around.?"

I breathed deeply, and my mind started to race. "Sadie, I must get Hannah out of New York, or this man will take away her child, put him in the foundling home, and throw Hannah in the street. I hope we still have time before that happens. Where can Hannah go? She has her family in Canada but is too ashamed to go there. I wonder if she can go to Palestine to Mischa's kibbutz. How can I get her there? First, I must tell her what happened. She needs to take her baby and leave."

"Look, Fannie, you can bring her here late tonight. Then tomorrow I'll be at the factory all day."

"Oh, Sadie, thank you, thank you."

"Meanwhile, maybe go over to the Henry Street Settlement House. They have been helpful to immigrants in trouble. Maybe they can tell you how to get Hannah on a boat to Palestine."

Diary, I arrived at Carmella's before Hannah came in and acted out how Esther was now ready for solid food. Carmella understood. When Hannah came in, she was surprised to see me without Esther. I told Hannah what Sadie had heard. Hannah gasped and clutched Daniel. I asked if she wanted to go to her family in Canada, or go to Palestine and meet up with Mischa.

Immediately she said, "Palestine. I can't face my family." Then she took all Daniel's clothes and rolled them into his blanket.

We walked to the Henry Street Settlement. I carried Daniel just in case anyone recognized Hannah. At Henry Street we talked to a helpful woman who spoke Yiddish. I explained to her that Hannah had to leave New York because her husband didn't want the baby. If Hannah wouldn't agree to give up her child, he'd kick her out. I told the woman Hannah has friends in Palestine, and she wanted to get on the first ship she could find. Hannah told the woman she could pay for her passage.

The woman left her desk and came back, saying there was a freighter ship going to Marseille the next day, and from there, Hannah could get a boat to Jaffa. Then we decided I would take Daniel with me back to Sadie's, and she would meet me in the morning, and we'd go to the dock.

We met the following day. Hannah was dressed like she was on the ship coming to America, in a plain dark blouse, a long skirt, and scuffed boots. Her long hair was no longer swept up but in a braid down her back. She carried a rucksack and held her yellow hatbox. I handed Daniel to her, and she handed me the hatbox. She explained that some of her fancy clothes were in it and told me to keep them, sell them, or give them away, anything I wanted. She said she was glad she didn't get rid of all her greenhorn clothes. We also planned I would write to Mischa tonight to tell him she was on her way to Palestine and ask if he could arrange for her to stay with her baby at Kibbutz Degania. When she gets to Marseille, she'll find a ship to Jaffa, then write him and let him know when she expects to arrive.

The freighter was already at the pier but would not sail for awhile. I got on with Hannah. A sailor led her to a tiny cabin on the lower level. Daniel began to cry, and Hannah started nursing and rocking him. He settled down. We sat still for some time, Hannah sobbing quietly.

"Oh, Fannie, I've made such a mess of my life. I never thought I'd end up in Palestine to be a farmer. From one day to the next, my life changes in ways I never imagined. But I have Daniel. He is family. Fannie, do you think I'm a horrible person for this mess I let happen? I wanted glamor, to escape poverty, and to be noticed, and look where it all led. If Daniel ever finds out about my past, he'll hate me. What will I do when he asks about his father? Will he ever forgive me? He was born because I became a whore."

Diary, I ached for Hannah. I wanted to tell her the whole story about what happened in Budapest. Without some luck, I could be in her situation.

"Hannah, I'm going to tell you something about me I've tried to forget and hide, even from myself. I've told no one the whole story. It haunts me. You are not alone in this. When I was sent to work in Budapest at an uncle's grocery store, the store went under, and my uncle sold me to a brothel."

Hannah snapped her head up and looked straight at me, saying, "No. I can't believe it."

"It's true. I did tell my sister, but let her think I escaped immediately. That isn't true. I was held captive there for months. It was the most humiliating experience of my life. I was forced by the head woman to dance and sing naked, and serve men. If I didn't, she threatened me with the police, the way Jack threatened you. And Hannah, like you, I hate myself for it, even though I was held hostage. Then one day, a boy about 16 came in looking scared. A couple of his drunken buddies dragged him in because he confessed, he had never been with a woman. He came into my room. We could hear his so-called friends outside saying crude things and egging him on. I said we didn't have to do anything. He could just stay awhile. He was a sweet boy and asked me about myself. I told him I was miserable and had been sold into this place. Then, on impulse, I asked if he could get me out and on the train to Lviv. From there, I would find some way to get to Bolekhiv. He thought for a while, then said his father had a horse and cart, and delivered bolts of cloth to a tailor. If I could climb out the window in the dark, he would meet me with the cart, and hide me under the bolts, then get me to the train station. This dear young man asked me if I had train fare. I didn't. He offered to pay for my ticket. So, Hannah, you see what an important part luck plays in how we survive." Tears streamed down Hannah's cheeks.

"Fannie, we're barely more than children, yet we have had the hardships of a lifetime. I'm so sorry for what you went through. Thank you for telling me. It's a gift, especially right now. I don't feel so alone."

"Hannah, I think telling you will help me live with the memory of that horrible time. At moments I wanted to tell Mischa, but I was too afraid; I depended on his loving and respecting me."

The freighter sounded its horn. Hannah, holding Daniel, and I embraced. Then Hannah said, "Fannie, I will always remember you. You are my dearest and most loyal friend. I think of you as a sister. I love you, Fannie."

"I love you, Hannah. Perhaps we are on this earth to rescue each other."

The horn sounded again. I rushed onto the gangplank. It was about to be pulled away from the pier. Watching the freighter sail out, I wondered how many times I would stand here and watch someone I love leave me. The boat was almost out of sight, and I heard myself say, "In this miserable world, you've still been able to love people. Although, so far, they all leave you."

I pulled my Esther's blue shawl tightly around my shoulders, touched the velvet bag holding Mischa's red ribbon and ring, and picked up Hannah's yellow hat box. Then I started back to Pike Street to write my letter to Mischa.

Chapter 19: Letters

Dear Mischa,

I hope this letter finds you and your Tateh well and settled in Kibbutz Degania. Your description of the tensions in Palestine are worrisome. Still, I hope you and your Tateh find comfort in being outside in clean air and enjoying the other people in the kibbutz who share your mission to build a Jewish nation.

Our friend Hannah is on her way to Palestine with her baby son, Daniel. I gave her your address to contact you. Like you, she left America suddenly and under great pressure. She sails to Marseille today. From there, she will find a ship to Jaffa, and write to you when she knows which ship and when it will arrive. I hope you can meet her at Jaffa and that she can stay at your kibbutz.

Sadly, Hannah became involved in an unhappy love affair with a married man who supported her and provided her with an apartment. When she became pregnant, he demanded that she put the baby in the foundling home, or he would kick her out on the street. She found a way to hide her baby and nurse him for several months, but soon there was a rumor she had kept and hid the child. She knew she had to escape quickly from New York if she and her baby are to survive. I hope she can find safety with you, at least for awhile, until she figures out her next step.

Mischa, it has been many months since I heard from you. I hope you are all right. I hold dear your ring and beautiful note, but I'm puzzled that you don't mention it in your letter. I feel at the mercy of my guesses why you haven't written. Are you sick or hurt? Have you forgotten me? Have you fallen in love with someone else? Mischa, please respond, even if the news is bad. I would rather know bad news than helplessly wonder.

Love to you and to your Tateh,

Fannie

Diary, after writing to Mischa, I felt weak and wanted to rest, but couldn't until I opened Hannah's hatbox. When I saw what was in there, I could see Hannah trying to leave behind her life in America. There were three fancy shirtwaists, two long skirts, her hat with the plume, a pair of elegant white leather shoes, and a hand mirror. We never had a mirror at home. There is a mirror at the public baths. I pass it by. A hand mirror—what can I do with a mirror? I put it down and tried on the shoes. They fit. I like the idea of walking in Hannah's shoes to remind me of the good things we share and the painful ones, too. They are too fancy for every day. I'll save them for the holidays.

I don't dare offer the clothes to Sadie. Maybe I'll put the shirtwaists and skirts in my rucksack. Perhaps the mirror too. What can I do with the hatbox and hat? Maybe I'll bring them to the Yiddish Theater, where Hannah worked for a while. Perhaps they can use them as props.

Later

Diary, I brought Hannah's hatbox and hat to the theater. They were glad to have them. Maybe she can find a theater group in Palestine. Perhaps they put on plays at the kibbutz. Maybe she has a future. Do I?

Weeks Later

Here is a letter from Mischa.

"Dear Fannie,

First, of course, we will welcome Hannah into our kibbutz. She has had a hard time. Here at the kibbutz, we accept people as they are. We don't ask what they had to do to survive.
Tateh is doing well here and sends you, his love.

Fannie, I'll try to be honest with you and tell you why you haven't heard from me. This is painful for both of us, but you deserve better than my hiding from you. I realize hiding is exactly what I've been doing. In your earlier letter, you called me heroic, or I try to be heroic. The last is true. I try to be heroic because, deep down, I know I'm a coward. I've been cowardly many times in my life. The first time I was cowardly with you was when I was too afraid to ask you to dance with me, and I asked Hannah instead. I know I hurt you then, and Fannie, I have now hurt you again and much worse. I should have found some way to send Tateh to Palestine and stay with you in America. I was desperate to protect him and responsible for what happened to him. Then I wondered whether I should leave Tateh here and come back to you. But here is the truth. Like

Hannah, I've gotten myself into a complicated situation. Hannah was a victim. I was stupid and weak.

Every night I keep dreaming of you and my poor dead Mama. When I wake up, I'm unsure who died, you or her. You and she melt together in my dreams. Poor Tateh doesn't know what to make of my sobbing.

The days are full of hard work, the evenings are social, or I have guard duty. Even so, I have never been so lonely. And here is the most troubling part to tell. I found comfort from a young woman in the kibbutz who reached out to me. As I write this, I ask myself, was it comfort or distraction from my pain? Maybe both. She is a perfectly fine woman. I respect her, but I don't love her. When she invited me to be intimate with her, I accepted, and she became pregnant. Despite the spirit of free-thinking here, the woman's family and the elders of the kibbutz pressed me to do the honorable thing and marry her. Your cowardly Mischa consented. I married her. We do have a lovely child, a girl we named Shira. I hold the secret that the name Shira was the Hebrew name I thought was right for you.

Fannie, Fannie, I wish I understood myself. I'm so sorry for what I have done, so sorry for what I have gotten myself into, sorry to lose you, and sorry for hiding from you. I don't expect you to forgive me. But Fannie, please know I loved you, and I love you. I feel unbearable shame for my cowardliness and unbearable sadness for what I allowed myself to lose in abandoning you. I grow physically stronger every day, but I know I am weak in will. I wish I had the strength to leave and come back to you. What is it with us? We are so bound to our parents, so bound to our tradition, so bound to what we are told is the right thing to do. And yet I try to be a freethinker. I am no freethinker. I am a pitiful child and a fool.

You should also know my Tateh is very disappointed in me and wishes you and I were together. He loves you as his own daughter. The *only thing that comforts me is that I experienced great love for you. I hope that can also comfort you. I will never forget you.*

Mischa"

Diary, I have never been so furious. Yes, Mischa, you are a coward! I will not be your puppet on a red ribbon! Pine for me all your life if that's what you need to do. Beat your breast in shame and remorse. The fact is, you're choosing your loveless life because other people say it's honorable. So much for your "Song of Songs" that sanctifies love between two people. So much for "Leave your father and mother and cleave to your wife." You are in love with other people's big ideas and ignore the truth of your heart and what we brought to each other. Yes, the desert is where you belong. Your heart is a desert.

Diary, after I wrote this, I went to sit on the stoop. I sobbed, wailed, and shook like Mischa did when I told him I couldn't go with him. I was flying apart. I let myself go. I must have been very loud because soon, I felt Sadie's arms around me, trying to hold me together. Every part of me ached, and I knew I could never erase the love I felt for Mischa anymore, then I could erase the love I still feel for my Esther and my Tateh.

Next Day

Diary, I am glad it's Sunday. Sadie will be with baby Esther all day, and I'll have time to think and pull myself together.

Later

I keep thinking about Mischa being intimate with the kibbutz woman. He wanted us to be fully sexual. I pretended I was a virgin, telling him I wanted to save our ultimate intimacy for marriage. That was a lie. The truth is I feared if he entered me, I'd panic with memories of the brothel. If I told him about the brothel, I feared he'd get rid of me and see me as disgusting.

Why am I so ashamed of being a victim? I feel terrible about stealing the dress, I feel terrible about betraying Sadie, but I feel much worse about being a victim of sex. Why? Why couldn't I believe that Mischa would hear my story with compassion like that boy who helped me escape? I needed Mischa too much. Needing him made me a coward.

If I had been fully intimate with Mischa and maybe gotten pregnant, would we be together now? Would he have stayed in America, maybe sent his Tateh alone to Palestine, so I could still help my family? Or would I feel trapped into going to Palestine and abandoning my family? I don't know.

There was a time I was sure it was *bashert* that Mischa and I were together. Now I see there was so much keeping us apart, our own weaknesses, the hard life in America, the fates of our families, the fire, and all that followed it. We are two cowards who love each other. We are separated twins.

That Night

A huge rat is chasing me. I'm terrified. I run and step on the hem of my dress. Falling, falling, I'm falling down an open cellar into a pile of stinking garbage.

Gasping, I woke up. Oh, my G-d, the dress in the dream was the dress I stole! I was wearing it. Didn't I get rid of it? Of course, I did. I washed it and fixed it, then sent it to Mama. Why did Mama get rid of me? Did she think I was a whore and a thief even before I was a whore and a thief?

Chapter 20: Body and Soul

October 1912

I received a letter from Hannah.

"Dear Fannie,

Thanks to you, I am safely in Palestine at kibbutz Degania. As we planned, Mischa met me at the ship in Jaffa. I'm living in a dormitory for women with young children. During the days, I work as a seamstress, making and repairing clothes for the kibbutz's men, women, and children. Daniel spends the day in the infant nursery. He is doing well, eating solid food, crawling, and pulling himself up to stand. I suspect his life here is not so different from the way it was in New York. Although he is in the nursery all day, he knows I'm his mother. He smiles and reaches out his little arms when I come to pick him up after work. He is my source of joy. Otherwise, I feel strange here. The people are kind, full of commitment, and high spirits, hoping to make a Jewish nation. I seem unable to join in. But Fannie, please understand I am deeply grateful to be safe and to have my son with me.

I realize I am avoiding writing anything about Mischa. He tells me he wrote to you about his marriage and baby. You must be heartbroken, Fannie. I only wish I could comfort you at this moment. I will tell you he is not the spirited Mischa we knew in America. His Tateh is now higher spirited than he is. Mischa is a reliable worker and someone who can be trusted to do his share in maintaining the life of the kibbutz. One thing worries me. He is always the first one to volunteer for night guard duty. He seems to have made friends with some members of the Hashomer.

Writing to you, Fannie, brings me comfort, even though my news is not all good. But then, isn't that our bond? We share the things that burden our souls. Let me know if it is better for you if I don't write about Mischa.

My family seems settled in Canada, and I have no plan to bring them to Palestine. I wonder if I will ever again see any of them.

There is one thing that pleases me. I asked whether the kibbutz was interested in having a theater program. They are, and I will begin with the children ages eight and above. We will write plays and put them on for the kibbutz.

Love to you,

Hannah"

Dear Hannah,

First, yes, I am in great pain about losing hope that Mischa and I will ever be together, but I would rather face the truth and try to go on with my life, just as you are doing. I feel lost here without Mischa and without you. Sadie continues to be very kind. Like Mama, she now suggests I think about getting married, and offers to arrange a marriage. Her Tante Malkah arranged her marriage to Itzhak, although I believe Tante Malkah now regrets the outcome.

It is good to hear your Daniel is doing well. Baby Esther is thriving too. I wish we could meet in the park and watch the two of them play.

I miss our efforts to speak English together. With Sadie's encouragement—or I could say, pushing—I'm going to the Henry Street Settlement and taking English lessons. There are some people my age there. We're not allowed to speak our own languages in class. About half of us are Yiddish speakers from Austria, Germany, Poland, and Russia, and the other half is a mix of Italian and Swedish. I read *The Jewish Daily Forward* in Yiddish—the *Forvertz*—then look at the American newspaper and try reading it out loud. I feel shy in the class. I don't stay after for the refreshments, dancing, and singing. It would make me miss Mischa too much.

I must tell you, Hannah, before you left America, I had read in the *Forvertz* about the ship Titanic hitting an iceberg and sinking. I worried about you at sea and held my breath until I received your letter saying you were safe. Reading about the Titanic brought back the horrors of the fire at the shirtwaist factory; people jumping to their deaths, the screams, the fires on board. I was shaking for days after.

I worry to hear Mischa is so quick to put himself in physical danger. I have learned that the worse he feels about himself, the more heroic he tries to be.

Hannah, you, Mischa, and I all carry the heavy burdens of our lives. We try to keep going. If I had to guess, I suspect I'm physically strong enough for my body to survive, but I am not so sure about my soul.

Love,

Fannie

Diary, I re-read my letter to Hannah. I was frightened when I saw the words about wondering if my soul will survive. I will keep going on, making money to help my family. That is my physical survival. But will I want to sing and dance, will I love the world, will I want to learn new things? Where is the girl from Bolekhiv, full of hope and curiosity? Where is the girl who loved loving Mischa?

I still wonder why Mama sent *me* away. I'm weighed down by what I've become in America. I'm ashamed of being a whore, a thief, a liar. I betrayed Sadie, I'm selfish and weak. These are all true since I left home. Is this the cost of survival? In Budapest, I was held hostage, but in America, I seemed to lose my sense of right and wrong. Is this what loneliness and fear does to people?

Diary, I had to stop writing here. I went for a walk. It was after dark. I sat on the stoop and remembered the times after shabes when Mischa walked back to Pike Street with me, and because it was too hard to part, we sat on the stoop and looked at the stars.

Later

Diary, after my walk, and remembering stargazing with Mischa, I could barely wait to come back to you and write the thoughts that follow.

I realize, even while trying to survive, I found a powerful loving friendship with Hannah and deep soul-mate love with Mischa. Loving them saves my soul. And while Hannah and Mischa are new in my life, I am sure that loving them comes from loving Esther and my family. So, whatever I have done, by bad circumstances or bad judgement, I'm capable of deep love and hope to love again.

Diary, I stopped short after writing the last sentence. "I'm capable of deep love and hope to love again". I must write to Mischa.

Dear Mischa,

Thank you for helping and welcoming Hannah. She feels lost right now, but I believe she well might make a meaningful life for herself and her child at your kibbutz.

Mischa, I feel compelled to respond to your last letter. This is not a letter of forgiveness. You have done nothing that needs forgiving.

We left our homes and came to America to save our families. Life here turned out to be rough and mean. Despite that, you and I found deep love and wanted more than anything to make a life together. When your Tateh was assaulted, you could not forsake him. My family survives because of the money I send them. We did what we believed we had to do at the time.

Recently, I feared while my body might survive, my soul would not, and this has prompted me to write this letter to you. I cannot allow my soul to die. Even as I write now, I re-live our shared tenderness and desire. I wish I had allowed us to fully consecrate and consummate our love. Isn't it what "The Song of Songs" teaches us as holy? My reluctance to allow us that holiness comes from a part of myself and my history I failed to share with you. I feared if you knew my secrets you would no longer want me. It is my cowardice. I wish I had dared to be fully honest with you, to trust you would still love me, and to have allowed myself to love you with every bit of my body and soul.

Mischa, I will never forget what we had together. It lives in my memory, in my heart, in the marrow of my bones. May the memory of our love for one another be for a blessing.

Go, Mischa, live and love your life. I will try to do the same.

Mazel tov on the birth of your daughter Shira.

Fannie

Diary, I have copied this letter onto your pages. I know in sad times, I will need to remind myself of what I felt and wrote.

Weeks Later

A letter from Mischa:

"Dear Fannie,

Thank you, thank you many times for your loving letter. We fell in love in America, the supposed land of freedom, but only now are we slowly learning the true meaning of freedom, to dare to be entirely who we are, with our strengths and frailties, and to trust in our love for one another, whatever is past, present, or future.

When I first saw you at the shirtwaist factory and again when you sang and danced at the settlement house, I saw your inner beauty rise like the sun. Yes, the memory of our love will always be for a blessing, whether we ever meet again or not.

Always,

your Mischa"

Diary, I weep but also breathe a deep sigh. Something calms and settles within me. I will place the small velvet bag with Mischa's ring and verses, and his letter, in my rucksack, now as filled with America as it once was filled with Europe.

END of PART II

PART III

Chapter 21: New Directions

February 1913

Diary, I continue to attend English classes at the Henry Street Settlement. English is difficult. There's no logic to it. We learned the words *rough* and *bough*. They don't sound like they are spelled, and they don't rhyme with each other, and there is no rule for figuring it out. I still can't make the ugly *th* sound. Iʼm too bad at this to speak with a native English speaker. I keep at it, as much for a place to go as anything else. Some people are friendly, and a few are around my age. I wish Hannah was here so we could practice together.

Otherwise, my life revolves around caring for little Esther, a sweet child, no trouble at all. She is almost a year old. I take her to Washington Square Park for fresh air and to play with other little kids. I keep thinking Hannah will come by and then remind myself she is in Palestine.

The other women with children are mostly English speaking. I suspect they think I'm Esther's mother, but I'm too shy to explain.

I'm becoming a good seamstress and hopeful it will be a better way to work than in a factory or doing piece work. People in the neighborhood bring their clothes to me for repair. One German Jewish woman who's been in America for a long time and lives uptown, asked me to copy a dress of hers. She likes the style and wants another like it. I took her dress apart, made a pattern out of newspaper, then sewed her dress back together. She brought me some beautiful green taffeta. The new dress turned out well. She was pleased and said she'd tell her friends about my fine work. I'm thrilled. It means I could do more interesting sewing than repair. Maybe someday I will design a dress.

I wrote to Rivka and Mama about my new skills. Here is Rivka's latest letter. I'm worried.

"Dear Fannie,

It sounds like you are on your way to becoming a real seamstress. When I told Mama about it, although she rarely smiles anymore, she did smile for a moment.

I know you read your Yiddish newspaper. Is anything being written about the increasing unrest between the Austrians and the Serbians? The conflict is an old one but now it is heating up. I find it too complicated to fully understand. It has something to do with Serbia wanting to take over all the Balkan countries. It is worrisome to us because there is talk of war. What does it mean for all of us here in Bolekhiv? Our brothers could be sent to fight. Fannie, I don't mean to alarm you, but I'm trying to think ahead and figure out what our family might face.

The neighbors say we might have to leave the area. Where would we go? I think Tateh had a cousin in Vienna. I know a girl from school who now lives in Lviv. Maybe I'm getting ahead of myself, but if we must leave our home here, I don't want to be surprised. Would Mama be willing or even able to move somewhere else?

Another thing I've been thinking about, Fannie, it is time we arrange a marriage for you. You will not have a dowry, so it needs to be someone who already has an income and can support a family.

I know I'm older than you, and tradition would have me marry first. But right now, I have taken over for Mama, who has sunk into such sadness she can barely care for herself, let alone the family. At moments, and this is very puzzling, she erupts into angry tirades, shaking her fist at no one in particular. That is not entirely true; I hear her cursing G-d in the middle of the night. Sometimes she yells and tears at her clothes. It is terrible to see. Kayla and Jacob both get frightened and cry. When Mama sees them crying, she cries too. The doctor came to see her but had no cure. He says she is suffering from melancholia, which can worsen while going through the change. It is terrible to be so helpless and watch someone suffer and rage. Little Jacob is so dear. He goes to Mama, pats her back, then rests his head on her lap. Mama responds a little. She pats his head.

Fannie, I don't mean to trouble you with all this sad news; I think I'm using this letter to get some relief and just do what needs to be done now. I hope you can bear to hear about all this.

Love to you from me and from all our family,

Rivka"

Diary, Rivka's letter fills me with worry and feeling helpless. However, I'm glad Rivka is telling me what is really going on. I'd rather know than guess. Maybe we are all getting more truthful.

As for getting married, I don't know what I think about it. Except for sewing, I don't know what I want. Taking care of little Esther distracts me from thinking about what's ahead.

An arranged marriage? I wanted to be with Mischa and feel full of love and desire. And what if war is coming?

Chapter 22: More Death, More Life

April 1913

Diary, I received an upsetting letter from Hannah.

"Dearest Fannie,

I am so sorry, but I have bad news. I have fallen ill, very ill. Mischa and his wife took me to the hospital in Jaffa. I have cancer of the blood, and they don't expect me to live much longer. I am growing weaker every day. My sister in Canada is on her way to Palestine to care for me. I know this is a shock to you, Fannie, and it is for me too. Is this unbearable punishment for my poorly lived life?

Fannie, I have a huge favor to ask you. Will you take Daniel? My sister already has six kids. I know people here in Palestine care about him, but I don't want to leave him in the kibbutz nursery. I want him to have a mother. I can't imagine a better mother for him than you. He is a beautiful and joyous child. If you can say yes, my sister will bring him to you. If you can take him, I will die knowing I brought a beautiful soul into this world and left him in the very best hands. I am asking you to make a huge decision without giving you much time to think it over.

I know you live with Sadie and Itzhak, so they will have to agree to it. Please write as soon as you can and let me know.

Your dearest friend loves you.

Hannah"

Diary, I had to sit for a long time and catch my breath. I tried to imagine being Daniel's mother. I was lightheaded and felt this could not be real. Hannah dying? Me, Daniel's mother? This was a strange dream I'll soon wake from.

The door opened and closed. Sadie was home from work. Esther called, "Mama, Mama," toddling at top speed toward Sadie, who scooped her into her arms.

I told myself to think only about the evening ahead. It was Friday. I prepared shabes dinner. Sadie will light the candles and say the blessing. Itzhak will say the prayers. We will eat. Sadie will put Esther to bed. Itzhak will go back to his books. Then I'll talk to Sadie. This is not a dream.

Later

After Esther was asleep, I showed Sadie Hannah's letter, Sadie gasped, and she, too, had to catch her breath. It was hard to absorb all that Hannah had written. Sadie's reaction brought me to the reality of it. I was losing Hannah forever, and at the same time she asked me to make a decision that changes the rest of my life.

Sadie continued to sit quietly, then looked directly at me and asked, "Fannie, what do you want to do?"

Thoughts galloped across my mind. If I agreed to be Daniel's mother, it was much more than a kind mitzvah to help my poor dying friend. Here I am, a woman without a husband, in a strange country where I barely speak the language. Here is a child, slightly more than a year old, who has no father and is about to lose his mother. I will uproot him from his home and from everyone he knows. I remember Hannah saying, "I have family with Daniel." If I take Daniel, then I will have family in America. Is that a selfish thought?

With a child in my life, should I agree to an arranged marriage? What man would accept a son who is not his own? What man would accept a son who is the child of a prostitute? Would I have to tell that truth to a possible future husband? What if no man will have me? I would be poor forever, and so would the child.

But I'm becoming a seamstress, and according to the well-dressed German woman, I do "fine work," and can keep working at home. I think I could make a life working, earning enough, and raising a child.

If I don't take Daniel, he will grow up in the kibbutz, maybe with one of the kibbutz families. That might be better for him. But that isn't Hannah's wish, and the kibbutz isn't safe from being raided, or even destroyed. Then I heard Sadie ask again,

"Fannie, what do you want to do?" Her voice startled me back to this moment.

I heard myself say, "Yes, I want to take Daniel and be his mother." But I was not sure whether I said it out loud or only thought it.

All at once I felt fullness in my heart and throat and heard myself cry out a loud sob. I felt full of Daniel and bereft that Hannah, my dearest friend, was suffering and dying.

Sadie waited for me to be calm. "So, Fannie, you will say yes?"

"Sadie, I'm scared, but I can only imagine saying, yes, I'll take Daniel, and he will be my son. My son, did I just say, my son?"

And then I was laughing and crying at once, and so was Sadie. Then Sadie pulled herself together to make a plan.

"I'll speak to Itzhak tomorrow afternoon after he returns from shul. It's good that tonight is shabes. Itzhak is always calmer during shabes. Tonight, he and I will be intimate, I hope. Then tomorrow, I'll tell him about Hannah's terrible illness and her dying wish that you take Daniel. G-d willing, he will say yes."

"G-d willing." I repeated, then added, "Oh Sadie, I thank you, Hannah thanks you, and I can imagine Daniel someday thanking you."

"Before you thank me too much, Fannie, let's find out what Itzhak will say." Then she added with a smile, "We will be crowded in this little home, but it will be full of the sounds of children. Daniel and Esther will be like cousins of the same age. They'll play together."

Imagining Daniel and Esther as cousins made me feel part of a family. That's what I want!

The Following Afternoon

Diary, I could hear Itzhak and Sadie talking behind the closed door of their bedroom, but I couldn't hear what Itzhak was saying. He said something in a loud voice, then I heard Sadie calmly talking more.

Itzhak still pays no attention to Esther. She toddles over to him and tries to get his attention. He ignores her. It's odd and sad. I can't imagine him agreeing to another child, not his own.

Esther was sound asleep in her little cot. She grew out of her cradle months ago. I tried to imagine Daniel now. He must be Esther's size. When I last saw him, he was still a little baby, sitting up but not yet crawling.

Sadie came out of their bedroom. I searched her face. She looked serious but not upset. "Let's talk on the stoop, Fannie."

I wrapped myself in my Esther's shawl, as much for comfort as for warmth. Sadie began, "At first, just at first, Itzhak said, no, he doesn't want someone else's child in his home. Then I told him it would only be for awhile because it was time to arrange a marriage for you, and I would see to it right away. He was pleased, and he agreed to Daniel coming if the two of you would leave soon. Fannie, I hope you understand I don't wish you to leave soon, but this way, at least you have a place here with Daniel until we make a match."

"I'm not surprised, Sadie. When I'm here in the apartment with Esther while you're at work, I know it makes Itzhak nervous. We don't want another dybbuk."

"I'll visit the matchmaker tomorrow and keep reminding Itzhak that you and Daniel will move out soon."

"But Sadie, when I leave, who will take care of Esther when you're at the factory?"

"Oh, right! I must figure that out." She thought for a minute. "Maybe my cousin Zelda will come. She often said being a midwife is not for her. I think Tante Malkah agrees. I'll ask Zelda if she wants to take care of Esther and do piecework."

Dearest Hannah,

News of your illness distresses me more than I can say. But yes, I will raise Daniel and love him, and always love you through him. You are as dear to me as a sister, and will always be in my heart and memory. I hope your gift to me of your beloved son will bring you some peace.

With much love,

Your Fannie

The Following Day

Sadie came to me saying, "I visited Tante Malkah to talk about making you a match. She thinks you should find someone from the upper West or East side because you have no dowry. They are richer than the people in our neighborhood or in Brooklyn. She has a friend Froma, also a midwife, who lives uptown. She's not a matchmaker, but as a midwife, she knows many families uptown and will see what she can find."

Chapter 23: Beginnings

May 1913

Diary, A few weeks have passed, and today I received a letter from Hannah's sister Leah.

"Dear Fannie,

I leave Palestine with Daniel tomorrow and expect to be in New York in a few weeks. When I reach Marseille, I will find a ship to New York, and will write telling you the ship's name and when it arrives. I will bring Daniel's clothes, but he may need warmer things in New York. Hannah still has some savings and insists that I bring the money to you so you can buy a cot for Daniel, and anything else you might need to take care of him. He is eating regular food and drinking diluted evaporated milk. I wrote to my brother, who has a pram his kids no longer need. I asked him to send it to you right away. When I return to Canada, I will look through the clothes my six kids have outgrown and send them to you.

Daniel is going through a difficult time. He did very well in the kibbutz nursery until Hannah fell ill. Since then, he has been clingy and often cries. This is all new, and I am sure once he settles down with you, he'll become cheerful again.

Hannah is very weak, but when she learned you will take Daniel, she breathed deeply and became peaceful.

Hannah was the wild one in our family, but she always had a generous heart. If it were not for Hannah working and sending us money, our family could never have moved to Montreal. I had hoped she would eventually come to Canada. We never understood why she chose to go to Palestine.

Daniel and I will not need to go through Ellis Island because we will travel second class.

Fannie, I look forward to meeting you at the pier. Hannah speaks about you with both love and great respect.

Yours,

Leah"

Three weeks Later

Diary, I arrived at the pier this morning. This time someone is arriving, not leaving! When I saw a woman with a small child walk down the gang-plank, I immediately knew it was them. Leah is older and heavier than Hannah, but the family resemblance is unmistakable.

She had a rucksack on her back and a large soft bag slung over her shoulder. She carried a small, delicately-made boy with wild, curly red hair and wide-set, big blue eyes. I waved, and she came right over to me. She leaned over to kiss me on the cheek. She had tears in her eyes.

"This is Daniel," she said. Daniel turned away and grabbed Leah with all his strength. I suggested we find a bench inside the waiting room and sit together. Daniel wouldn't look at me for a long time.

Leah and I continued to speak. She told me how Hannah put on plays with the children of the kibbutz. One was an original play where each child described their journey to Palestine from their home in Europe.

Leah asked me about my journey and life in New York. When Daniel heard my voice, he became curious. Still clinging to Leah, he cautiously turned toward me. Then I spoke directly to Daniel, telling him about his "cousin" Esther, just his age, who I knew would want to play with him. Leah said, Daniel enjoyed being with other children.

We sat together for a long time. Daniel relaxed onto Leah's lap, facing me. I had brought some peeled apples and gave him a piece. He ate it right away and reached for another piece. We went on like this for awhile. Soon I stretched out my arms to him. He came to me and kneeled in my lap as though he needed to study my face. Finally, he sat in my lap, facing Leah, frequently turning to look back at me. He reached out his hand, and I put a piece of apple into it, then reached out his other hand and I put another piece in that hand. He leaned back, gnawing on his apple pieces from each hand.

I asked Leah how she was getting back to Canada. She said a boat leaving soon would take a route up the Hudson River. She looked at the clock in the waiting room and said she had to get to the boat soon, and needed to buy her ticket. It was time to part.

Leah leaned over and kissed Daniel and kissed me. She handed me the big soft bag saying, "Mischa will write to both of us about Hannah." Her eyes were full of tears again. Leah and I held each other's hand for a moment.

Then I said to Daniel, "Let's go and find your Cousin Esther." I stood up and turned Daniel toward me so I could carry him. He strained his head around to look at Leah. When he saw her walk away, he pushed against me, reaching out to her, first screaming, then crying with huge sobs that shook his little body. I had to hold him with all my strength. He is small for his age, but strong. I sat back down with him. He cried until he must have exhausted himself completely and fell asleep, his warm damp face nestled into my neck.

Together, we walked back to Pike Street. Everyone was home when I arrived. Itzhak rushed away into the bedroom. Esther raced over to look at the "baby." I asked Esther, "Is it all right if Daniel sleeps in your cot for a little while?" She thought about it and shook her head a firm "No!" So, Sadie and I settled him on the sofa where I sleep. We put chairs up against the sides so he wouldn't fall. I told Esther this was where Daniel would sleep every night until he got his own cot. She approved.

Daniel woke up after everyone else had gone to bed. He let me change him and hungrily ate the soup I fed him with a spoon. He drank a cup of milk, then looked confused, even stunned. Again, he wanted to kneel on my lap and not only stare at my face but pat it. As he touched the parts of my face, I said, "Eyes, mouth, ear," and so forth. Then he cried again. I wrapped him up in my Esther's shawl, and we walked in the neighborhood.

Daniel cried and cried; I didn't know a child could cry so loud and for so long. Again, he exhausted himself, but this time didn't sleep, although his head rested on my shoulder.

We walked and walked for a long time. I started to sing a Yiddish lullaby, *Shlof Mayn Kind.* He must have known it because his voice, without words, joined mine. We went on like this, repeating it many times. Then, without even thinking about it, I swayed and turned in rhythm to the song. Then out of Daniel came the sweetest sound I had heard since time with Mischa: he giggled. And then I giggled. Then I cried, and Daniel kept giggling. We returned to Pike Street. Still holding Daniel, I stretched out on the sofa, and we both fell asleep.

The following morning, I woke before Daniel. I realized that last night was the first time I sang and danced since Mischa left.

When Daniel woke, he again looked confused, but was quiet. Esther, of course, was right there, showing Daniel the pots and pans she likes to play with. Daniel watched cautiously but didn't join in right away. Soon he picked up a pot and a spoon, and Esther changed her mind about sharing them.

I took them both to the park, a child on each hip. It felt good. When we returned, I saw Sadie had found a cot for Daniel and placed it right next to Esther's cot. I put them in their own beds, and they both slept soundly.

Before going to bed, I wrote to my family about Hannah and Daniel. I don't know what they will think. Rivka is raising Lazar and our little Jacob and Kayla, and I will raise Daniel.

Chapter 24: And Another Beginning

Summer 1913

Diary, my life is changing so fast. Sadie told me today that Froma, Tante Malkah's friend, will come Sunday to meet me and ask questions so she can find the right husband for me. When I heard this, I felt a big wave of sadness, knowing yet again, Mischa and I will never be together. There was no one I could talk to, so I wrote to *A Bintel Brief.*

Dear *Bintel Brief,*

I am a woman who left my home in Galicia when I was around 16 years old and came alone to America. I fell deeply in love with a fine man, and he with me, but for reasons I will not describe in this letter, we will never be together. Yet I realize I love him still.

My good friend here in America is arranging a match for me. I cannot imagine ever loving another man the way I loved my first. I am afraid I will always unfairly compare my husband with my first and only beloved. Is it fair to commit to someone who will always be in second place and perhaps who I will never love?

I look forward to your wisdom on this question.

Yours,

A Seeker of Advice

"Dear Seeker,

The ability to love another is a great human gift, and the ability to fall deeply in love is G-d's blessing. But to pine forever for what you have lost and not take hold of life and move forward is folly.

Arranged marriages are a long tradition for our people, but remember, these days, you don't have to accept the first man introduced to you. You will know when there is someone you can imagine loving. We cannot see the future, but we can make reasonable guesses with good information. Think about his character and what he values. This will help to guide you.

With hope for your future,

Bintel Brief"

If I ever dare to love someone again, I won't do what I did with Mischa, hide my past for fear they'll get rid of me. If they don't want me, I'd rather know it right away than always worry they'll learn the truth. If no man will have me because of my past, I have Daniel. I have the possibility of well-paying work I enjoy, and I already know I can make friends. I'll learn English, and can make a life here for Daniel and me, with or without a husband.

On Sunday, Tante Malkah, and her friend, Froma, visited. While we drank tea, Froma asked about Daniel. I explained, "My dear friend, also a greenhorn, became involved with a married man and gave birth to Daniel. She decided to move to Palestine with Daniel and raise him there. But a few months after they arrived, she fell ill and learned she would not survive. Her family could not take him, and she asked if I would raise him. I agreed. Sadly, she is now near death."

Froma did not look pleased. She asked, "Do you have a dowry?"

"No, but since coming to America, I gained skills as a seamstress, and hope to earn and work from home."

Froma kept on with her questions. "And your family?"

"I'm here alone. My family is in a shtetl near Lviv. I send them a little money each week."

Froma sat back in her seat, sighed, squinted her eyes, and studied me. Soon she sat forward again, saying, "This will not be easy. You're a young woman with no family here, with a child who is not your own. While you may have some skills and can earn a small living, you will need a match with a man with reliable work who can support you, especially if your seamstress ambitions don't work out." She asked, "Are you a religious girl?"

"I grew up in a religious home, but since coming to America, I'm not religious. However, I observe Jewish traditions and know the prayers. I know how to keep a kosher home and observe the holy days."

Froma tilted her head from side to side with her eyes closed. She was taking it all in. Then sighed and said, "Well, I'll see what I can do." She looked like she was thinking about something, then looked straight at me, saying, "Fannie, Will you consider a man older than yourself?"

"How much older?" I asked.

"Maybe ten or 12 years older."

"Yes, ten or 12 years older is all right, but not more. I don't want to be a widow too soon." Hearing myself, I realized I already felt like a widow.

"I think we have more of a chance with someone older and well-settled, who needs a wife and mother for his children now."

A few weeks later, Sadie came to me saying she had heard from Froma. "Fannie, his name is Marek Horvath. He's 29 years old, a widower from Pest, and has a three-year-old daughter. He came to America eight years ago and worked as a tailor. Now he owns a small tailor shop on the Upper West Side and lives with his daughter in an apartment on the Upper East Side. His wife died a year ago in childbirth. He is ready to move on and find a mother for his daughter and a wife for himself. Fannie, I think you should meet him." I agreed.

The Following Sunday

Diary, what a day. Froma and Marek arrived this afternoon. Sadie set the table with tea, almond cake, bread, and cheese. She sat at one end of the table with Esther on her lap, and I sat at the other end with Daniel on mine. Froma and Marek sat on either side. Itzhak left the apartment.

Froma began by introducing Marek and repeating the information she had written in her letter. She then repeated the information I had given her. Then Froma left, and Sadie took Esther out to play, so Marek and I were alone.

Marek is a handsome man with thick black hair, brown eyes, and a well-trimmed beard without payes. He has a broad chest and shoulders. He looks his age except for his eyes, which seem older and saddened by suffering.

Daniel sat on my lap and stared intensely at Marek. Marek first addressed Daniel, saying, "Daniel, you look like a fine boy, serious and curious. I'm Marek. I have a little girl, Adela, who is three years old. She is staying with her Tante right now. Maybe you will meet her."

Daniel kept staring at Marek, but soon settled back into my lap and reached toward the loaf of bread. Marek cut a piece and handed it to him. I could feel Daniel's body relax. He became thoroughly interested in his crust of bread.

Then Marek addressed me. "Fannie, what questions do you have? I will try to answer them."

"Please tell me about your family."

"Most of my family are still in Pest. I came to America eight years ago with my older brother, who, sad to say, died of pneumonia five years ago. We were doing alright in Pest and saw the trip to America as a big adventure. When we arrived in New York, we worked as cutters and pattern makers in a tailor shop. We had already had some experience working in Pest. My mother, father, and two young sisters are still there. They are managing so far. I want them to come to America because I worry about the treatment of Jews and the possibility of war, but they are reluctant to leave."

Marek paused, then said, "I would like to tell you about my dear wife. We married soon after my brother died. I was lonely and wanted to find a wife. My friend, also a tailor, introduced me to his sister, Miriam. We married, and a year later, we had Adela. Miriam became pregnant again. She went into labor in the seventh month, and both she and the child perished. It's been a difficult time for Adela and me. Like your Daniel, Adela too is a serious child and curious. She is a loving girl who helped her Tateh get through this sad year. I want to see her laugh again."

When Marek said he wanted to see Adela laugh again, I told him the story of carrying Daniel through the streets as he cried and cried.

"When I started singing to Daniel, he became quiet. When I swayed to the rhythm and turned around with him, suddenly, he laughed. It was the sweetest sound I ever heard. He still doesn't laugh much, but it's beautiful music when he does."

Marek tilted his head to one side, looked searchingly at me, then said, "Tell me about yourself."

"I come from a shtetl south of Lviv. We were a family of eight children, but like you, Marek, I, too, lost a sibling. After I arrived in America, my twin sister died in Bolekhiv of a bad heart. Then my Tateh also died." Marek folded his hands under his chin listening intently. I went on.

"I came to America alone, hoping to work and earn enough to bring my family over. I first worked for my uncle and his wife, but they didn't pay me. I was lucky to find a home with Sadie and Itzhak. Itzhak is my mother's cousin. Daniel's mother, Hannah, who I met on the boat coming over, helped me find work at the Triangle Shirtwaist Factory."

Marek interrupted, his voice urgent, "Were you in the fire?"

"Yes, but with help, I got out. Of course, then I needed to find work. Sadie asked if I would do piecework and care for Esther in exchange for living here. Sadie is like an older sister to me."

I knew what I was saying to Marek was the bare bones of my truth. I thought, if this moves forward, I'll tell him much more.

Marek knew from Froma how I came to be raising Daniel. He asked how Hannah was doing.

"Sadly, I hear from people in Palestine she is close to death. She was always helpful to me. When she asked me to take Daniel, I didn't realize how much joy this small boy would bring me. He is a gift."

Marek and I spoke more about how Adela and Daniel had too much of life's sufferings for children still so young. Marek asked, "Would you like us to meet again?"

"Yes, I would."

"Do you think you might enjoy going to the Yiddish Theater on Sunday? The play will be a musical with singing and dancing."

I felt excited, and the words popped out, "I would love it!"

"Then that's what we'll do." Marek smiled.

Before he left, Marek asked if he could say a blessing over Daniel. Slowly and gently, Marek cupped his hands around Daniel's head. Daniel turned up his gaze, meeting Marek's, and Marek recited in Hebrew the sabbath blessing over the children of the family. My eyes filled with tears. It was just like my Tateh and Mischa's Tateh had blessed all the children present.

Chapter 25: Light

The Following Sunday

I dressed up wearing one of Hannah's shirtwaists; after all, we were going to see a play at the Yiddish theater where she had worked.

Marek met me at Pike Street, and we walked to Houston Street. It was a warm summer evening, the sun just beginning to set. When we crossed the Avenue, Marek offered his arm. I took it. He's a solid man. I could feel the firm muscle of his forearm and the smooth gabardine of his jacket. I wondered if he had made his jacket.

We sat in the balcony. I looked at the crowd of people. Most were nicely dressed. The lights dimmed. The play opened with a young man singing *A Brivele der Mamen*. When he finished, there was a brief sigh in the audience, then wild cheering and clapping that went on for so long, the actor agreed to sing it again. I wondered how many people in the audience also left their mothers behind in Europe, probably never to see them again.

After the actor sang the second time, Marek and I turned to each other. We both wiped away our tears, and then, I didn't understand it, but we laughed.

The play continued, with more songs and some dance. I loved every moment. I could see from the side that Marek sometimes looked at me.

An actress came onstage, playing a young person leaving home, angry that her family would not accept her new American ways. I was stunned to see her wearing Hanna's big hat with the plume and carrying Hannah's yellow hatbox. First, I thought, "How can that be?" Then I remembered bringing the hat and hatbox to this theater's costume department. I burst into tears and ran out into the theater lobby. Marek followed, looking puzzled and worried. We sat a moment on a velvet bench while I gained some control of myself.

"Marek, when Hannah, Daniel's first mother, left for Palestine, she handed me a yellow hatbox filled with some of her things, and a hat with a plume. This shirtwaist I'm wearing tonight was in that hatbox. Hannah told me to do what I wished with her belongings. She wanted to be an actress in this Yiddish theater, so I brought some of her things here for their costume department. Marek, that actress we just saw was carrying Hannah's yellow hatbox and wearing her hat. When I saw her come onstage, I could only think, because Hannah is near death, I have the joy of Daniel."

Marek sat by quietly listening. He asked no more. Soon, Act One was over, and the crowd filed out for the intermission. I felt calm again. Marek asked, "Fannie, we can leave if you wish or go back to watch the play. Whatever is best for you is best for me."

"Please, let's go back inside. I was loving it. But the sudden reminder of Hannah came as a shock. I'm fine now." We returned and stayed until the end.

Afterwards, while walking back to Pike Street. Marek asked, "Would you like to meet Adela? Perhaps we might take Daniel and Adela to Washington Square Park next Sunday."

"Yes, I want to meet your Adela and I want Daniel to meet her too. I was told Daniel enjoys being with other children of all ages. He did well in the nursery in Palestine."

I thanked him for the evening, and as I climbed up the stoop, I looked back. Marek stood for a moment waving, then walked toward the subway stop. I guess my outburst in the theater didn't send him running.

I soon fell asleep, thinking about the firm feel of Marek's forearm and his sleeve's smooth cloth.

I'm looking into a lighted window, a home, maybe on a stage. Vague. A family—voices. Who are they? What are they saying? The light is golden—candles? A setting sun?

Chapter 26: Laughter

The Following Sunday

Diary, we met at the fountain in the park and then walked to an open grassy space, where we sat on a bench. Adela held tightly to Marek's hand. She is three years old, the same age as my little sister Kayla when I last saw her. I felt a wave of homesickness.

Adela is a pretty child with long, dark hair and large brown eyes. She is slender and maybe tall for her age. She carried a tightly rolled-up blue and white tablecloth. Marek explained that the tablecloth is her favorite plaything. She stared at Daniel, who sat on my lap. I said to her, "This is my little boy, Daniel."

She nodded and clearly said, "My name is Adela." She turned to Daniel, asking, "Do you want to see what I do with my tablecloth?" I don't know what Daniel understood, but he nodded, "Yes."

Adela went onto the grass and, holding two sides of the cloth, billowed it up in the air and let it fall softly to the ground. She did this many times until Daniel wiggled off my lap and toddled over to joined her. She handed him an end of the cloth, and Daniel followed her lead, billowing it and allowing it to drift to the ground. Then Adela turned to Marek, calling him, "Tateh, Tateh, make me the sky!"

Marek went to her and, taking the two ends of the cloth, billowed it high in the air. Adela ran under it, laughing as it fell over her. "Tateh, again!"

Marek threw the cloth up in the air but in a different place, so Adela had to run to get under it. Daniel stood watching. Marek offered to lift Daniel up and run under it with him, but Daniel came to me. I picked him up, and he pointed to the cloth. I asked him, "Do you want to go under the sky too?" He nodded and pointed. Then Marek picked up Adela and, with a one-arm thrust, sent the tablecloth flying high, and the four of us stood under it while the "sky" Marek made drifted down upon us all.

"Again, Tateh, again, make me the sky," called out Adela, and the four of us did this more times than I can count. By then, we were all laughing.

We returned to the bench and rested for a while. I brought pieces of peeled apple, Daniel's favorite, and we all had some. Soon Adela again said, "More sky Tateh." Then she turned to me and instructed, "Now Daniel goes with Tateh, and I go with you." She reached for my hand, and Marek reached out for Daniel, who went easily into Marek's arms. I wondered if a man had ever held Daniel. Maybe Mischa in Palestine. Another wave of longing came over me.

Marek sent the "sky" soaring, and we all ran under it many times, and laughed while it floated down, enclosing us in a blue and white cloud. Marek and I were soon out of breath, but the kids kept playing. Adela lay on the grass, rolling herself into and out of the tablecloth, then helped Daniel to roll himself into it. They were screaming with delight as Adela led the way.

Marek turned to me on the bench and said, "Fannie, I want to make the four of us a family. I hope you do too. I want to ask Itzhak for his blessing. Will you be Adela's mother and my wife?"

I answered, "Yes, and will you be Daniel's father and my husband?" Looking at Marek, I felt myself full of yearning. I yearned for all I lost:

my Esther, Tateh, Mischa, and my family. And at this moment of this joyous day, I longed for all I might yet have.

Chapter 27: No More Silence

We were getting ready to leave the park when Adela turned to Daniel and said, "Daniel, we had fun. Goodbye, I'll never see you again."

Marek said to her, "Do you want to play with Daniel again?" Adela nodded and said a firm, "Yes."

Marek said, "Then we probably will see Daniel and his Mama again."

Marek and I planned he would bring Adela home to her "Tante"—not really her aunt but a neighbor who helps Marek care for Adela. After Adela was asleep, he would come back so we could talk. The night was warm, and we planned to sit outside on the stoop.

Marek returned at around nine o'clock. The streets were quiet, and for a few moments, we were both silent. Feeling very nervous, I took a deep breath and began.

"Marek, soon after I came to America, I fell deeply in love with a young man only a little older than myself. He also worked at the shirt-waist factory. I think we both assumed we would marry.

After the fire, our lives changed. He and his father went to Palestine. He begged me to go with him and make a life together. I didn't go, thinking my obligation was to work and send money to my family. I couldn't earn money in Palestine. As time has passed, I realize it was not the only reason I didn't go. I didn't go because I was afraid if the young man ever found out who I was and what my life had been before we met, he would reject me. I kept silent, and my silence made me afraid. Marek, if you and I are to marry and make a family together, I need to know you accept me as I am or if you can't, we part right now."

Marek looked surprised but remained quiet. He gestured for me to continue.

"I was never sure why my mother sent me to America. I have older brothers. Why did she send me, and why alone? Did she know something about me I didn't yet know? Did she want to get rid of me? She told me she was sending me because I was clever. I don't know if I believe that. First, she sent me to Budapest to work at my uncle's store. When the store went under, my uncle sold me to a brothel where I was held hostage. I told my mother and my sister, and I immediately ran away..."

I paused. "That is not true. It took me a while to escape, and in the meantime I was forced to work there. Then my mother sent me to New York to work for another uncle, who sold used clothes. He refused to pay me unless I let him use my body. I ran away but had nowhere to go. I was so angry before I ran away from my uncle that I plunged my hand into his disgusting pile of old clothes and stole a dress. I was ready to be a beggar and live on the street. Hannah, Daniel's mother, saved me, helping me to be safe and to get a job at the shirtwaist factory. So, I need you to know I have been a prostitute and a thief. Although I'm young and single, I'm not a virgin bride."

I was out of breath and stunned by my own words. Did I just say all this to a man who thinks he wants to marry me? But then I went on as though it didn't matter anymore. I told Marek that Hannah, too, was forced into prostitution.

Diary, I was out of breath, coughed and sobbed. I want the life I think Marek is offering. He is a kind man, a good father. I thought I had wrecked that chance.

Marek was quiet for awhile but never took his eyes off me. Then he said, "Fannie, we live in a world that can be cruel. We choose life and do what we can to survive. Trying to survive can be ugly. I was not going to tell you something about myself because I, too, am afraid you will not have me. But you're right. We must come to one another, taking ourselves and each other as we are, not who we wish we were. I know that men often prey on young women who come alone to America. Your story, and Hannah's, is the story of so many girls sent away by their families when they are too young to make that journey safely, especially if they are sent alone. Your so-called theft surely was fury at your horrible uncle. What's important is you wouldn't succumb to cruel treatment, even if it meant becoming a beggar. In the brothel, you were a victim but eventually figured out how to escape. You found ways to survive that didn't harm anyone. But I need to tell you, my truth. While women are preyed on, men get violent."

"I was 16," he continued. "We lived in a basement apartment. I came home from school, my father and brother were working at the shop, and as I walked in, I heard my little sisters crying and my mother screaming. An intruder, a big man, was holding down my mother and trying to rape her. His back was to me, and because of the screaming, he didn't hear me. I grabbed a knife from the table and drove it with all my strength into one side of his back. I pulled it out and thrust it again into the other side of his back. He staggered up, blood pouring out of his back and mouth, and he ran into the street, where he collapsed. I think I killed him. Thank G-d no one saw him come from our apartment. My mother sent me to be with my father and brother. The police came to all the apartments in the neighborhood, trying to find out what happened. When they came to our place, my mother had already cleaned up the blood. They saw only a woman and two little girls, so they left and kept searching."

"Fannie," Marek said, "I lied to you when I said my brother and I came to America for an adventure. We came here fearing I would be caught and sent to prison or worse. As a Jew, they would never let me off because I was protecting my mother. But I live knowing I likely killed someone, and if it happened again, I would do the same thing. I never told my wife. Only my family knows. Fannie, will you still have me?"

Diary, what I said next came out suddenly like a sob or a laugh. "Marek, Marek, make me the sky."

Marek opened his arms, and I moved close to him. He enveloped me. I let myself lean onto his broad chest while feeling the strength of his embrace. How can anything that feels so right be wrong? We stayed like this and were both sobbing. I think we both felt, at last, a new life can begin.

Before we parted, Marek said, "One more thing Fannie. Athough I was raised as an Orthodox Jew, I no longer welcome the strict rules or mysticism of orthodoxy. This past year, I found comfort at the Reform synagogue, Temple Emanu-El. Out of respect for Itzhak and Sadie, I think we should marry at Itzhak's synagogue, but I would prefer to remain a member of Emanu-El. Fannie, would you be willing to come to my temple?"

I asked, "Would your temple disapprove of our hugging on the stoop?"

He laughed and said, "No, they would sanctify it."

So, I said, "After we marry, I'll come with you to your temple."

We parted, hugging again, this time with joy.

Chapter 28: At Last

Diary, Sadie was waiting for me when I returned. When I told her Marek and I would marry, she was thrilled. The strength and joy of her hug almost lifted me off the ground.

"Fannie, I think he's a good man. I'm so happy for you." She sat at the table with a pencil and paper, and started making a long list of wedding plans.

I said, "I'll make my wedding dress."

"Good! Now Fannie, be sure to let me know when you have your next monthly. We go to the mikveh seven days after, and four days after is the wedding date."

Sadie made the invitation list. "We'll invite Tante Malkah, Zelda, and, of course, Froma, who made the match, and my friends from the factory. I'll write to Marek and get his list. I know a group who play klezmer music, so we'll have dancing. Guests will bring cakes and wine. It will be a big party. Think about who you want to want to invite, Fannie."

Sadie's question startled me. I realized all the people dear to me since coming to America are now in Palestine. Then there's Feter Oscar and his family. I won't invite them.

Before going to bed, I wrote to my family and Mischa, telling them the news. In my letter to Mischa, I expressed how I hoped this letter would arrive soon enough for Hannah to know her son would grow up in a family with a good father. I added how someday I would tell Daniel about his brave mother, who, knowing she was dying, wanted only the best for him.

It was bittersweet to write to my family. Here I am, finding a husband and a new life in America. Rivka, who is older than me, is single and burdened with all the care of the children, and of our Mama, who withdraws more and more into herself. Of course, I will still send money to them, maybe more if my sewing goes well. I think Rivka and Mama will be relieved to know I'm married, especially now that I'm Daniel's mama.

The next evening, Marek returned to ask Itzhak for his blessing to marry me. Sadie, the children, and I went out in the hall while the men spoke.

Marek told me, Itzhak never looked at him. When he asked for his blessing to marry his cousin, Itzhak first nodded yes, then said "Yes, yes" and fled from the room.

Marek must have been very sure Itzhak would say yes, because he brought four yards of beautiful, soft white cotton for my dress.

While waiting for the right time to go to the mikveh, I made my dress. It is fitted on top with long, loose sleeves and a long full skirt that billows like a cloud when I walk. Down the front of the bodice, I embroidered two entwined leafy vines in blue thread. They are a symbol of marriage and of twinship. I need to feel Esther's presence at my wedding. I'll also wear her shawl. And I'll wear the white leather shoes Hannah packed in the hatbox.

Three Weeks Later

Diary, Sadie, and I went to the mikveh today. A kind-looking older woman, the rabbi's wife, the *rebbetzin*, met us at the door of the synagogue. Sadie waited outside for me. The rebbetzin and I went to the basement to a washing room. She handed me a long white cotton gown saying, "You are to completely undress. There is the sink with plenty of soap and clean rags. Wash yourself all over and very well, then put on the gown. I will wait outside the door. Take your time. Remember, you are preparing your body to be loved by your husband."

When she said this, I felt tingles up my spine and into my legs. I took her advice and washed every part of me carefully.

I noticed there was a long narrow mirror on one wall. I looked at myself in the mirror. I'm slender, but I see now that my hips curve gently outward. My breasts are bigger than I remember them, and rounder. I had washed my hair in the sink. It hung in long blond curls below my shoulders. I wonder if Marek, being Reform, will expect me to wear a hair covering?

I had brought my rucksack containing Hannah's beautiful shirtwaist and remembered I also kept Hannah's hand mirror. When I took it out, I realized I could use the mirror to see my back. I've never seen my back. The image I saw startled me. Except for the color of my hair, I could have been looking at Esther's back. Even though we did not look exactly alike, we were always the same size. I was looking at me, but I saw Esther. It was shocking, but also right to have her with me now. Then I thought of something I never thought before. Everyone in our family has brown hair and brown eyes, except Esther and me. Esther was the only redhead, and I'm the only blonde. I have blue eyes. Esther had green eyes. Why were we different from everyone else?

The rebbetzin was waiting, so I quickly shook out Hannah's shirtwaist, hung it over the back of a wooden chair, and then slipped on the long white gown. The rebbetzin and I walked down another flight of stairs to the mikveh. The mikveh was somewhat like the communal baths, but smaller. The water was very clear. The rebbetzin gave instructions.

"Now, Fannie, this is what will happen. First, you'll take off the gown, then enter the water. I will say three prayers. After each prayer, you're to immerse yourself completely."

Holding a metal railing, I let myself down the three stone steps into the water. The water was pleasantly warm and as high as my waist. I went to the middle of the mikveh and faced the rebbetzin.

In her first prayer, she asked G-d for my health. And when she paused, I sank beneath the water. I kept my eyes open and could see my hair floating around me.

The second prayer was for my fertility, and how I should bear many children. Again, I plunged as deeply as possible, imagining our new family growing even bigger.

The last prayer was for peace. As I dropped below the surface, I imagined my family in Bolekhiv and hoped they would be safe.

The rebbetzin handed me a towel to dry myself, telling me to put the white gown back on and follow her to a room where she would further prepare me for my wedding. We entered a small room with two chairs.

She spoke of the sanctity of marriage and how G-d made our bodies to be enjoyed. "You should become well acquainted with all the parts of your body that make you a woman, a woman who desires her husband, and a woman who wishes for children. It is sanctified that your husband shall bring forth your feelings of desire for him. Then you will look forward to the night of the sabbath, and many babies will grow in your womb. It is your husband's duty to awaken your womanly sources of pleasure. However, during these four days before your wedding, learn to know your body. Your husband may need some guidance from you. Doing this will bring special joy to both of you every shabes eve and will bless G-d for his bounty."

I returned to the washing room to get dressed. The rebbetzin's voice and words were a lullaby, a soothing balm. The clear, warm water of the mikveh felt like a cleansing from the brothel in Budapest, from the ugliness of Feter Oscar, and from my theft as well. Perhaps it was a second cleansing. The first was my telling it all to Marek. Maybe I was cleansed, not of those bad experiences—they happened and will always have happened—but of my shame. I felt like dancing.

Before leaving the washing room, I took Hannah's mirror. I carefully looked at all the different parts of me I had never looked at in a mirror. My body parts have different feelings. I can imagine spending the rest of my life living in this body home, my body home.

I dressed, admiring how I looked in Hannah's shirtwaist. Then I packed up my things, and left the mikveh. Sadie was waiting for me.

Chapter 29: Under the Chuppah

August 25, 1913

Dear Diary,

Yesterday was my wedding day. Oh Diary, I can't believe I'm the same person as the girl who left Bolekhiv, the girl who escaped from Budapest, the girl who lived on the Lower East Side, fell in love, and lost my twin, my Tateh, my lover, my friend...and yet, and yet, I feel a sense of peace I've never known. I will tell you about our wedding, but first, I must tell you that Marek brought me home to his apartment uptown on Lenox Avenue. It has indoor plumbing! It's small but clean and cozy. Adela has a room of her own but is happy to share it with Daniel, who she loves to boss around.

Marek and I have our bedroom, and there is a kitchenette with a stove, and an icebox. I live in a palace!

Marek's tailor shop is on the West Side. He has two sewing machines and says I can work either at the shop, or he'll bring a machine home. Sadie wants me to take the machine of hers I was using and call it a wedding present. So, I will have a sewing machine at both the shop and home.

Our wedding was at Itzhak's shul, the Eldridge Street Synagogue. First, there were two parties, one for women, and one for men. The women sat me in the center of the room as though I was on a throne.

They danced and sang for me as I watched. We could hear the men singing and dancing in the next room. Afterwards, everyone went outside to an open yard in the back of the synagogue. The wedding ceremony was outdoors at night, under the stars. Dozens and dozens of candles were lit and carried by the guests. At one end of the open yard stood the rabbi. Marek's friends, a married couple, walked on either side of him and accompanied him toward the *chuppah*. Marek carried Adela in his arms. Sadie and Itzhak walked on either side of me, and I held Daniel in my arms. Now here comes the surprise. When I arrived under the canopy, I looked up. Marek had arranged for it to be made from Adela's blue and white tablecloth. I think I burst out with a cry of joy. Adela had given Marek permission to borrow it, but only for awhile. Adela, standing next to Marek, pointed to it, saying, "Look, Tateh. This sky doesn't fall down on us!"

Daniel pointed to it, too, saying, "Look, look, Mama." He called me Mama for the first time...as though, somehow, he understood this was the first moment of his being in a family.

The service began. Sadie took Daniel and Marek's friends, each held Adela's hands. When we came to the part of the service where I walked in a circle around Marek, I took Daniel back in my arms, and reached out my hand to Adela. The three of us circled Marek, husband, and father, seven times.

Marek placed the ring on my finger. His friend handed him a wine glass wrapped in a cloth napkin. Marek stomped on the glass with his right foot, making a loud pop. The guests yelled, "Mazel tov!" and we were married.

Sadie embraced me. Her cousin Zelda came up holding little Esther, who reached out her chubby arms to me.

Then came the party, men, and women together. There was a table spread with bottles of wine and cakes. The klezmer musicians played, and a big circle of people danced the hora. Some of the men danced a wild kazatsky.

Adela saw to it that Esther and Daniel made a circle with her and tried to get the two toddlers to dance. Soon they were all in a pile on top of one another, giggling and screeching. The three were great entertainment, especially for the older guests who sat clapping and cheering them on to try again.

Marek came up to me, and the klezmer band played a Viennese waltz. Marek is a strong dancer. When he took me in his arms, and we moved to the rhythm of the music, I felt our embracing bodies create our home.

Someone brought us two glasses of wine. Marek raised his, first to the crowd and then to me, shouting, *"L'chaim!"*–to life!

Chapter 30: Home

September 7, 1913

Diary, it's been two weeks since our wedding. Marek and I are making a good life together. Mornings, Adela, and Daniel stay with their Tante Ida, Marek's neighbor, while I help Marek at the tailor shop. In the afternoon, I'm with the children. When I can, I try to do some sewing at home, mostly repairs, but dressmaking orders are slowly coming in.

On Sundays, we want to spend time with Sadie and Esther at the park and sometimes have their family here for shabes. Also, I'm meeting some of Marek's friends and their families. My life is full of people.

None of the married women in Marek's synagogue wear head coverings, although they may wear hats. Marek said I could cover my hair when we go out if it feels more comfortable, but he asked me not to at home. He says he loves my hair and wants to see it. I decided I would only cover my hair when we visit Sadie and her relatives; otherwise, I won't.

Marek's shul is so different from Itzhak's. I like these differences, but it takes some getting used to. Men and women sit together. The rabbi greeted me and welcomed me to the congregation. He even shook my hand.

We'll keep kosher since it is what we're both used to. It reminds us of our family life at home in Europe. It also means kosher friends can have meals with us here.

Marek is not religious, but he loves some of the Jewish traditions. I'm not clear about what I am anymore. Was I ever religious? I followed what I was taught and didn't think about it. In America, it became difficult to follow what my family did. I wonder if Esther studied Torah to find out what it means to be religious.

I think Mischa embraces being Jewish as a people he belongs to, but sheds the spiritual part. Marek's rabbi speaks of peace and the brotherhood of all people. We recite prayers in Hebrew, and G-d is mentioned. Still, it feels very different from what I experienced at Itzhak's shul or even the one my family went to in Bolekhiv. I can't imagine Marek's rabbi exorcizing a dybbuk.

Moving uptown from the Lower East Side is like coming to a new country. I'll continue to study English. Marek has learned a lot of English. He said he had to if he wanted to run his tailor shop. I need to know English if I'm going to help him in his shop and become a dressmaker.

Along with *Forverts*, Marek and I attempt to read what we can in the American newspapers. His English is way ahead of mine, but he is always willing to translate for me. We try to keep up with what is happening in Europe. We both worry about our families, wondering how much danger they face if war comes.

Family life here makes me feel connected to my life in Bolekhiv. The time I spent living on a fire escape seems very long ago. I could have been living on the street if it hadn't been for Hannah. Now I live with my own new family in a comfortable apartment. I feel safe here with Marek. The days move forward with some predictability. However, what happens with our families in Europe is always a shadow of worry crossing our minds.

Next Day.

Diary, sadness, and joy always seem to be bundled together. This morning, I received a telegram. I was terrified to open it. I had never received a telegram before.

September 8, 1913

"SAD NEWS. HANNAH DIED TWO DAYS AGO BUT SMILED WHEN I TOLD HER DANIEL WOULD GROW UP WITH YOU AND A GOOD FATHER. LETTER FROM ME ON THE WAY. MISCHA."

I knew it was going to happen. Still, I'm stunned. I looked over at Daniel playing with a cup and spoon, pretending to feed himself and making *mmmm* sounds. He is always busy with something. I could spend the day watching him go from one fascination to another. The other day he discovered that doorknobs turn. He toured around the apartment, reaching for doorknobs and laughing as he grabbed and turned each one, then made the tour again.

When will he be ready to hear about Hannah, her devotion to him, her life, and her death? For now, watching Daniel comforts me.

Two Weeks Later

Here is Mischa's letter.

"Dear Fannie,

Mazel tov on your wedding. Marek is a fortunate man to have found and married you. My Tateh sends his love. He is doing well and is more robust than he has been in a long time. He says we should have come to Palestine first, not to America.

We all grieve for our Hannah, but she was at peace when she died, knowing Daniel and you are part of a family.

I have become more involved in the workings of the kibbutz and want to take a leadership role here as soon as the elders think I'm ready to do so. With my beloved daughter Shira, the future of Palestine, and our kibbutz, my life is whole again with a sense of meaning and purpose.

I think of you often and expect I always will. Our life paths parted, but our time together will always be for a blessing.

Mischa"

I'm glad Mischa wrote as well as sending the telegram. I'll always feel blessed by what we found with each other. He filled me with some of his courage and spirit and maybe some of his so-called free-thinking. I hope Marek has similar feelings about his poor wife, who died so young. May her memory be for a blessing.

January 1914

Diary, many months have passed since I wrote to you. I am content. Marek and I work side by side in the shop. I'm beginning to use my English with the customers and when shopping for food. I'm always surprised when I'm understood. Also, I'm getting more orders to make dresses. Bringing our families to America begins to be a real possibility.

Our customers are mostly German Jews living on the Upper West Side who came to America many years ago. They don't like to speak Yiddish. But if we can't communicate in English, I speak German with them.

The best day of the week for Marek and me is Sunday. The four of us sit together at lunch, and when the children finish eating, they play together near the table. They both call us Mama and Tateh now. I have not become pregnant, and when I raised this worry with Marek, he answered, "Of course, if you became pregnant, I would be thrilled, but we already have a family together, a beautiful son and daughter."

At that moment, Adela and Daniel were playing with the blue table-cloth, and Adela said to Daniel, "Let's make us the sky." I turned to Marek and said,

"Marek, you are my sky." He replied,

"Fannie, dearest, If I am your sky, you are my stars."

Soon, the children needed to nap. Marek and I went to our bedroom. We embraced, and I felt desire and passion that I never believed I would ever feel again.

Chapter 31: The Library

Dear Diary,

A public library nearby has a collection of Yiddish and German books. I took out a copy of *Das Kapital* by Karl Marx because Mischa used to talk about it. It's difficult to understand, but I read a little of it at a time and will keep renewing it so I can continue to read it. It feels good to read again. I want to read all the stories by Sholem Aleichem again because they remind me of my life in Bolekhiv. I also took out a copy of *Grimm's Fairy Tales*, which I loved as a girl.

The librarian, Miss Kaminski, is a friendly woman who is always willing to help me find things. She speaks Yiddish but also encourages me to speak English with her. She asked me what I liked to read. I told her I enjoyed meeting people in stories and learning about their lives. She thought I might enjoy reading a current writer, Thomas Mann. She suggested a story called "Tonio Kroger." Tonio comes from a very different life than mine. Still, like me, he knows what it's like to be lonely and tries to understand other people and himself. He also has a passionate nature.

Miss Kaminski and I sometimes talk. When she was little, she came from Lithuania with her parents and went through the New York public schools. After 12th grade, she went to a place called Hunter College to study literature. She always loved to read and thought she might become a schoolteacher but became a librarian instead. She likes to work with people of all ages.

She asked about my family. I told her about my brothers and sisters, but especially about my twin and my Tateh, both having died after I came here. I also told her about Mischa. She was once engaged to be married but sadly, her fiancé died.

I also told her about Marek, Adela, and Daniel, and the family we now make together. She took me over to the children's section and gave me a book of English nursery rhymes for the children. She thinks reading them aloud and hearing the rhymes and rhythms will help our English.

When I returned to the library, Miss Kaminsky suggested I take out a copy of *Shakespeare's Sonnets*. She said I would not understand them for awhile but to stay with it and keep re-reading them. She said, "First, you will enjoy the music of the words. As you start to understand more, you will enjoy how they speak about the ways we love one another. Start with Sonnet 31."

We went to a corner of the library where she read Sonnet 31 out loud. I could hear the music and wanted to move to the sound as she read.

Thy bosom is endeared with all hearts,
Which I by lacking have supposed dead;
And there reigns Love, and all Love's loving parts,
And all those friends which I thought buried.
How many a holy and obsequious tear
Hath dear religious love stol'n from mine eye,
As interest of the dead, which now appear
But things removed that hidden in thee lie!
Thou art the grave where buried Love doth live,
Hung with the trophies of my lovers gone,

Who all their parts of me to thee did give,
That due of many now is thine alone:
Their images I loved, I view in thee,
And thou (all they) hast all the all of me.

After reading in English, Miss Kaminski found a German translation so I could begin to better grasp what Shakespeare was saying. She handed me a pencil and paper and suggested I copy the original English version right there in the library. She explained that in Shakespeare's time, English was a little different. For example, the words *thou* and *thee* have a similar meaning to the word *you*, and the word *art* is the same as *are*.

As I wrote the words, I wondered if this was how Esther studied Hebrew and the Torah. When I reached the line, "Their images I loved, I view in thee," it surprised me to remember how I sometimes thought of Esther when I felt entwined with Mischa, or how I think of Sadie as my Rivka in America. And Marek too. He's a bit of my Tateh, a bit of Mischa's Tateh, and yes, he is Mischa too.

Shakespeare's words brought me these thoughts! He was talking to me from hundreds of years ago in a language I barely understand! I felt tingling and excitement all over my body. I wish I could tell Hannah. Will someone new become my Hannah?

Chapter 32: Joy and Shame

July 1914

I just received a letter from Rivka. I'm shocked and confused. The news will take a long time to settle in me. It's like finding the missing piece of a puzzle.

"Dear Fannie,

I have so much to tell you. You may already know that the heir to the Austrian throne was assassinated by a Serbian in Sarajevo. What I have to say is all against the background that Austria is now at war with Serbia, and more and more countries are choosing sides.

Aber and Yehuda have both enlisted in the Austrian army. Aber wants me to take Mama and the kids to Vienna, where we have cousins we've never met but who are willing to take us in. Aber thinks Vienna is safer than where we are. He suspects there will be battles close to Bolekhiv, and the army will take our house as a shelter for the troops. If we stay here and the military occupies our house, he thinks we will all be put into one room and only allowed to use the kitchen for part of the day.

Mama is in terrible shape and refuses to go to Vienna. She wants me to leave her here to die. She says, "I don't want to die in a place I don't know and among strangers." She will not listen to reason, turns her back, and faces the wall.

That is only the background of what I must tell you. For many days Mama lay in her bed turned toward the wall and, except for refusing to come with us to Vienna, said nothing. I brought her food, but she took only the smallest amount. Then she became restless, twisting and turning in her bed, crying out sometimes. Moaning through the night. This went on for days. Then one night Mama called me in a voice stronger than I had heard in a long time. I will try to write everything she said as best as I can remember. She made it clear she wants you to know this.

'Rivka, I have something to say that you must tell Fannie.' Her face was bright red, and she had to catch her breath many times. But her voice stayed strong as she grabbed onto my arm and looked intently into my eyes.

'After Yehuda was born, I was in my early 20s, and your Tateh worked for the salt mine. My Mama and Tateh were both sick and died that same year. I was full of grief and loneliness. The house needed a lot of repairs, so Tateh hired a young man, a Polish carpenter, to do the work. This young man came every day. At the end of each day, we sat at the table and had a cup of tea together. He wanted to talk to me. I liked his company and was flattered. He was smart. He was on fire with curiosity, ambition, and flaming red hair. He read everything he could find in our small town. He hoped one day to go to Budapest or Vienna and attend University. He wanted to be a doctor.'

Here Mama paused. She dropped her head, looked away from me, cried for a few minutes, and then grabbed my arm tighter and continued.

'He thrilled me with his high spirits and intelligence.' She paused again, 'I confess, we briefly enjoyed a love affair, and I became pregnant. The doctor suspected twins. I was not sure they were his until I saw the two baby girls at birth. They were both so fair, and I knew for sure when I saw the blond and the red hair. Meanwhile, my Polish lover left

for Vienna, and we never met again. He never knew he left twin girls behind.' Here Mama broke into painful sobs.

'Your Tateh was a good and wise man. I loved him as one loves a dear relative, but I knew passion for the first time with my sweet carpenter.' The blood rose again in Mama's cheeks, and she almost shouted, 'Fannie should know her vitality and spirit and Esther's intelligence came to bloom because they were conceived in great love and passion with a brilliant and handsome man with flaming red hair. I never regretted my love for him. I only regretted betraying your good Tateh. Fannie and Esther were my greatest joy and greatest shame. I loved my twins, but I also feared them. They held my secret. I continued to love my dear carpenter, although we never met again. Was Esther's illness and death my punishment from G-d? I fear I sacrificed Fannie to her hardships in America. I'm tormented that I sent her away.'

Mama was out of breath, and she lay back on the bed. Soon again, she grabbed my arms and pulled herself to sit. 'If Tateh ever suspected, the babies were not his, he kept it to himself. I suffered alone with my secret. His silence was his devotion and protection of our family. If he acknowledged it, he knew he would have to divorce me. Also, Tateh loved his twin girls. He never questioned their fair coloring or differences from the rest of the children. They may have been his favorites. Had he been with us, I suspect he never would agree to send Fannie away to work.'

Here, Mama loosened her grip on my arm, fell back onto the bed, then turned again to face the wall. Since then, she has not said a single word.

Oh Fannie, I wish I could be with you while telling you this. It is all so shocking and sad that Mama had to live with such a tormenting secret. I can't imagine our family without you and Esther. May her memory be for a blessing.

But Fannie, it is hard to imagine our Mama, betraying our Tateh. And yet, we have you and we had our beloved Esther. That is all good. But Mama's suffering and maybe Tateh's too is such a heavy sadness. I wish you were here so we could talk and comfort each other. Of course, I will not tell the others. I don't think Mama wants that. I hope unburdening herself to me, and through me to you, brings her some peace.

Because of the War, Aber says we won't be able to send letters unless we are in the military or sending mail to a soldier. I will keep Aber up to date, and hopefully, he can get news to you.

Love to you and to your dear family in America,

Rivka"

Diary, I'm overwhelmed. War, Mama wanting to die, and this secret! It's too much. We all knew war could be coming. I knew Mama was withdrawing into herself more and more; but this secret! I can't believe my Tateh isn't my father. I knew Esther, and I were somehow different from the others, but I saw it only as our coloring and special bond.

What went through Mama's mind when she looked at us, and Tateh's too? Now I know Mama thought about us differently from the others. It wasn't just being a blonde or a redhead.

The part of the letter I keep going over and over is where Mama says, "Fannie and Esther were my greatest joy and greatest shame. I loved my twins, but I also feared them. They held my secret." I can't believe Mama really feared us, but if there's any truth to it, is that why she sent me away? It's painful to think Mama believes Esther's death was punishment.

I wish I could tell Mama, although my life has been hard at times, I'm glad I was born. I wish I could tell Mama, "I, too, have known great passion. It's a gift, although it can also bring pain."

Chapter 33: War

Late July 1914

A letter from Aber and Rivka:

"Dear Fannie,

Rivka and I have been exchanging letters. She wanted me to send this letter onto you.

Aber

'Dear Fannie,

Things are moving fast here. Russia has joined Serbia. Twenty Austrian soldiers have taken over our house. Lazar, Kayla, Jacob, and I are taking the coach-train to Vienna from Lviv. Aber arranged for an ambulance driver to bring Mama to Lviv. A nurse will meet her, and they will take a sleeper train to Vienna. We will meet at our cousins' apartment. The apartment will be crowded, but Aber thinks we will be safe there. He will be sending you letters from now on.

Love to you and to your dear family in America,

Rivka'"

A Week Later

I received a letter from Aber.

"Dear Fannie,

I am so sad to tell you our Mama died in the ambulance on the way to the train. She fought against us with strength I could not believe. She looked so frail. She kept repeating, shouting, 'Leave me here. I'm only a burden.' Then she reached into the waist of her skirt, pulled out her shroud, and covered her face. We began to drive, and in a short time she stopped breathing. It was heartbreaking to send her body to Vienna. But there she will have a funeral with the family present and will be buried in the Jewish cemetery. I feel such grief that our Tateh and Mama are not together in our cemetery in Bolekhiv.

I will do my best to keep writing to you and let you know what I hear from Rivka and the little ones.

As you know, Yehuda and I are now in the Austrian army, and to our surprise so is Lazar. Lazar, only 17, kept talking about wanting to join the army. When he saw the crowded Vienna apartment, he enlisted, probably lying to the recruiter about his age. More underage boys are enlisting. There is an upsurge of loyalty to Franz Joseph.

We were lucky to be born in Austria. Our Franz Joseph has been good to the Jews and allowed women to attend school.

I send my love to you, dear sister, and I hope to meet your American family someday.

Aber"

Diary, how many losses can I bear? Marek was at the tailor shop. Adela and Daniel were playing. I wrapped Esther's blue shawl around the three of us. They thought it was a cuddle game. We held one another, and I had a surprising thought. We are three people who lost the mother who gave birth to us. My orphaned sisters and brothers are now in the middle of a war, and I have never felt as safe as I do now.

When Marek came home, I showed him the letter. We scooped up the children, and all held tightly to one another.

Marek's family will stay in their apartment in Budapest. It is probably the safest place for the moment, although hatred of Jews is worse than ever, and food is scarce. Hopefully, this war will be over soon.

I'm getting more dressmaking work. We could bring both families over now if it wasn't for the war. May we all live long enough for that to happen.

August 1914

A letter from Aber.

"Dear Fannie,

Rivka, Kayla, and Jacob are settled in Vienna, living with our generous and welcoming cousins. I hope Rivka's letters get through to me. As best as I can, I will keep you updated on them.

Now Germany is allied with us. Russia is mobilized and on the move invading Galicia.

Rivka is worried about Lazar in the army. He's had his head in books most of his life, but there was no stopping him. Yehuda, Lazar, and I are all in the same unit. I'm glad about that. They gave Lazar a job as a cook, keeping him at some distance from the fighting. He has never cooked a meal, but I think they realized how young he is, and he will learn. Maybe he will be able to get a job quickly if we come to America.

Maybe this will be over soon. Maybe, maybe, maybe!

Love to you and your family,

Aber"

Late September 1914

I received another letter.

"Dear Fannie,

Our family left just in time. In early September, at Lviv, or what the Germans call Lemberg, we took a beating from the Russians. They far outnumbered us. Thank goodness we three are all still safe. The Russians now occupy the city. Our unit has been sent up into the mountains to fight. Winter is no time to be in the mountains, but that is how it is.

I'm amazed your letter got through to me. I don't know how long the mail will work, but so far, so good. I am glad to hear you are doing well and learning English. Your sewing business sounds promising.

Fannie, being in the Austrian army is confusing and sometimes chaotic. As you know, Galicia is made up of many different people, Poles, Hungarians, Romanians, Austrians, Czechs, Jews, and Germans, and we all speak different languages. Our commander only speaks

German. I can translate for the Poles because, in our shtetl, we all spoke German and Polish as well as Yiddish.

The Jews in any of the nationalities who speak Yiddish make out all right because they mostly understand German from Yiddish. For once there is an advantage to being Jewish. But anyone else who doesn't know German or Yiddish must follow the rest of us blindly. There are many accidents where people start running in the wrong direction or shoot at someone in their own company. We are a living Babel.

Then there is the fact that many of the Russians are Jews. How is it that one Jew must shoot and kill another Jew? It's an abomination! The only way to get through this is to try not to think about it and just obey the commander. Still, at night I imagine my supposed Russian enemy davening one morning and getting killed by me, another Jew.

Jews are spread all over the world. We have been on the move forever. Whether we live in France, South America, Russia, China, or Galicia, being Jewish is the only constant thing about who we are. When countries are at war, we are forced to kill our cousins and brothers. How can G-d allow such an atrocity?

And if that is not bad enough, both the Germans and the Russians are suspicious of Jews, so on both sides, we get accused of spying for the other side.

Fannie, I'm sorry to write to you about these things. I find, however, that putting these thoughts into a letter and sending it off sends it away from my mind for a while so I can do the job we must do here.

I hear from Rivka that Britain and France have joined the war to support Russia. But that is all I know. I have no big picture of this war, only what is in front of us today. If you learn more about what is going on, please write me about it.

Remember, if you don't hear from me don't assume the worst. We may be fine, but the mail may not get through, especially in the moun-

*tains. In case something awful happens to us, the Austrian army has
your address and Rivka's too.*

Love and Shalom,

Aber"

I don't remember Aber being as emotional and expressive as in this
letter. And he, like me, finds it helpful to write about what we're going
through. We have more in common than I ever realized. We have all
been through a lot. I hope I can get to know this big brother better.

His letter reminds me of Mischa's letter from Palestine. The hatred
in this world, even between Jews, is never-ending. Yet I have also known
the most tender beauty in nature, poetry, and between people. Adela and
Daniel can get angry and even fight, but mostly they keep reminding us
of goodness and love. What turns people to hatred? How does it happen?

March 1915

Diary, Aber wrote to say all three brothers were hospitalized in Vienna,
but all will survive. Aber has severe frostbite and must have some toes
amputated on both feet. Yehuda was shot in the shoulder and now can't
raise that arm. Lazar has typhus but is recovering. Many don't, but youth
and care help. It may mean Aber and Yehuda will be discharged; Aber
because his balance is affected and he needs to use a cane, and Yehuda
because he can't handle a weapon now. It's unclear whether they will
send Lazar back to his unit. So far, they are alive, thank G-d.

Chapter 34: Almost Safe

January 1916

For many months I received no word from my brothers but also nothing from the Austrian army. Today, finally, a letter arrived from Aber in Vienna.

"Dear Fannie,

I have very hopeful news. Yehuda, Lazar, and I were discharged from the hospital and the army. We were sent "home" to Vienna. We live close to Rivka in a nearby apartment building where we rent a room from an elderly couple. We help them in exchange for rent. Lazar and I can earn a little by going from apartment to apartment and offering carpentry and repair work. We must borrow tools but there is a comradery among people as we all find our way through wartime. I'm lucky to still work my trade, even with a limp and a cane. Yehuda cannot join us because of the injury to his arm, but like Tateh, he is good with numbers and is trying to find work as a bookkeeper. He can still write because his injury was to his left arm.

Food is scarce and costly. But we are managing with cabbage and potatoes and sometimes black bread. Yehuda uses his cooking skills to make different dishes using only cabbage and potatoes. He will do fine as a professional cook once this war is over.

> *I was able to travel to our home in Bolekhiv. It is in ruins. After the Austrians left, the Russians moved in and first wrecked it, then abandoned it when it was hit by mortars. I wept when I saw our old stove standing outside in the snow.*
>
> *I learned that Jews who remain in our area of Galicia are treated horribly by the Russians. Thank goodness we left.*
>
> *This war has thrown all the countries of Eastern Europe up in the air, and who knows where they will land and who will be running them. Bolekhiv could end up being part of Germany, Poland, or Russia, depending on who wins which battle. If this war ever ends, what will this part of the world look like?*
>
> *Rivka has been amazingly strong, caring for and protecting Kayla and Jacob. You would not recognize the little ones. Kayla is eight years old. Rivka has taught her to read. And can you believe Jacob is six and wants to help me do carpentry?*
>
> *L'Chaim and love to you and your family,*
>
> *Aber"*

I'm so grateful my brothers did not get killed in this war. But why must survival so often have such a high price, losing your home, your toes, a useless arm, disease?

November 21, 1916

Diary, today I read that Emperor Franz Joseph died. I grew up believing we Jews in Austria were lucky to have Franz Joseph. We still had our share of being targets of anti-Jewish feelings, but not like some other countries. I can't imagine what lies ahead for the Europe I knew.

Diary, I barely write to you these days. Even with the war going on, my life is full and happy at home. You helped me through so many painful times. You have been a loyal friend I could always talk to, everything I worried about, and all my joys. As lonely as I was at times, you were and still are always ready to hear what is happening or what I'm thinking.

I have a dresser drawer filled with your notebooks. I even have the copies of *Forverts* I wrote on. They are carefully wrapped in pillowcases to keep them from crumbling. Maybe someday the children will be interested in them.

I still read *A Bintel Brief* and usually think the advice is quite good. I remember reaching out to it and feeling reassured by the response.

The librarian, Miss Kaminski, or Rachel, as I call her now, is a true friend to both Marek and me. She is somewhere between Rivka's and Mama's age. She is a loving "Aunt" to the children (not a "Tante"), always bringing them new stories in Yiddish and English. Adela and Daniel speak better English than I do.

And still another exciting thing: not only am I making dresses for customers, sometimes I'm designing them. One customer is an actress at the Yiddish theater, and she told them about me. I'm now making costumes for them. I wish Hannah could also be working at the Yiddish Theater. Just imagine Hannah as an actress and me as a costume designer. How we would talk about our time together when I slept on her fire escape and how we miraculously survived the fire at the shirtwaist factory.

Chapter 35: To Life!

April 1917

Diary, great news for Marek and me. I'm pregnant, and the doctor suspects twins. We waited for so long. Marek is filled with joy but also terrified that I, like Miriam, his first wife, could die in childbirth. We agreed I would be cared for by a doctor at Bellevue Hospital and give birth there.

If we had decided to have the babies at home, I would have asked Tante Malkah to be the midwife. She understands our choice of the hospital, knowing how Marek suffered when his wife died. Tante Malkah will come after my delivery to help me settle into nursing. I will be like my Mama, nursing twins, and in a way, like Hannah too. When new people come into my life, they often remind me of people from the past.

As I write this, I remember Rivka's letter about Mama's revelation at the end of her life. It is unsettling to think that the children I bear will not be related to my Tateh, but to another man I never knew. Then I remember how much I love our Daniel and our Adela, and we share no inheritance in the bodily sense.

My body is changing. I can feel it happening. I wanted to see the changes. I now have a full-length mirror near my sewing machine so customers can look at themselves in their new clothes. One afternoon when the little ones were napping, I took off my clothes to look at my body. I was amazed at my large breasts and darker nipples. My belly is like a little haystack. Marek loves to stroke it and talk to the babies.

Then I took out Hannah's hand mirror. I turned to look at my back in the mirror, but I didn't see Esther this time. If Esther had the chance to become pregnant, would she look like me, with fully rounded hips and buttocks? I ached, wishing she and I could be pregnant at the same time.

Do I look like Mama when she carried us? If Mama saw me now, she would be reminded of having twins and a heavy secret? Will I also have twin girls? I'd always worry about losing one.

With the coming babies, Marek thinks we should find a bigger apartment on the Upper West Side, closer to the shop. He says we can bring our families to America once this war is over. Our business does well. I'm so glad to be able to write these words. Yet, I remember how survival so often depended on money and how angry I felt when I had none.

Early October 1917

Diary, I am very pregnant now; I'm huge and the babies are so active. The doctor says there is no question, I'm having twins. He hears two heartbeats.

We are getting ready to move to an apartment on the West Side. As I went through our belongings, I found my rucksack on the top shelf of our bedroom closet. Once it held everything I brought from Europe but is now filled with mementos from my American life.

I kept Hannah's mirror in the rucksack and one of her shirtwaists. The little black velvet bag holding Mischa's ring, with the red ribbon and writings from "The Song of Songs" is also there. I took out each object, cradling them in my hands and tried to name what I felt. Hannah's and Micha's faces floated before me. For Hannah, I longed for our friendship and thought she would always be in my life because she gave birth to my beloved Daniel. For Mischa, I was surprised to feel no yearning. Instead, I felt gratitude for how he awakened me in many ways. I believe loving Mischa opened me to love Marek.

October 30, 1917

Diary, baby Miriam and baby Simon were born yesterday. The babies are both healthy, and so am I. The birth went well, but I missed Tante Malkah, although she is here now helping me.

Miriam is named for Marek's wife and Adela's mother. Simon is for my father, Shimon. May their memories be for blessings.

We live on the Upper West Side now, near the Hudson River. Adela, Daniel, and I often go to Riverside Park, where they like to play. Sometimes Sadie and Esther come uptown on the train to meet us, or we go downtown and join them at Washington Square Park.

Adela is seven years old in second grade in the local public school. Daniel is five and is in kindergarten. Both children easily shift from Yiddish to English and English to Yiddish. Adela is teaching Daniel to read. Life is good. Marek and I work together, raise our family together and feel blessed.

So, Diary, dear and trusted friend, I will write again but not as often. I am so content to have a somewhat predictable life filled with the extraordinary, ordinary pleasures of work and home.

Late December 1917

A letter from Aber:

"Dear Fannie,

Vienna is in turmoil. The workers have taken to the streets, protesting the monarchy. I am sure you know America just declared war on Austria-Hungary. Does it mean my family here in Vienna and you and your family in America are enemies?
The world is spinning out of control. Where will it end?

If this war ends, I hope to come to America, and so does Rivka, with Kayla and Jacob. I am not sure about Yehuda and Lazar. Both have fallen in love with gentile Viennese girls. Rivka and I don't interfere because they are both happy. We can't take that away from them, after all they lost and have been through.

Our childhood in Bolekhiv feels like lifetimes ago.

Love to you and your family,

Aber"

Dear Aber,

I am thrilled you, Rivka, Kayla, and Jacob, plan to come to America. If Lazar and Yehuda change their minds, we can bring them too.

Since America declared war on Germany, the streets here are full of young soldiers who all seem happy and excited to be sent into battle. I don't understand it. Maybe they've never seen brutality, destruction, and missing body parts.

We send our love to all of you and dream of our reunion.

Fannie

October 29, 1918

Diary, Miriam, and Simon are a year old today. They are sturdy, healthy, fearless, and determined to explore every corner of the apartment. They are almost ready to walk but prefer to crawl, going so fast that I must run to keep up with them. Why bother walking when crawling gets you where you want to go faster?

We have a double pram, and I take them to Riverside Park. There are some flat grassy places where they have more freedom. When they are tired enough to be still for a while, they babble together and seem to be answering each other. It sounds like ordinary language, but it is only their language. They are very funny, but I must not laugh. They seem very serious as they "talk" to each other. I wonder if Esther and I did this. I'll have to ask Rivka and Aber if they remember it. Probably not. They were too young.

December 1918

Here is the letter from Aber I've been waiting for.

"Dear Fannie,

On November 11,1918 the war ended for Austria, albeit with complete defeat.

Rivka and I, with Kayla and Jacob, are ready to come to New York. As I expected, Yehuda and Lazar will remain in Vienna with their sweethearts. Both plan to marry as soon as they can.

Will you send a letter sponsoring us, and we will apply for immigration. It is not as easy as it was when you left. I think the fact that I served in the Austrian army and was wounded will help. Probably being Jewish helps too. They are glad to be rid of us.

Love to you and your family,

Aber

P.S. Did you know we are no longer Austrian? At the end of the war, we were briefly Ukrainian, and now we are Polish. Yet again, I am grateful we grew up in Austria."

Dear Aber,

Of course, we will sponsor you and set up work for you and Rivka here in the tailor shop. I will go to the immigration office tomorrow.

Your decision to come to America is a dream come true. You will meet my American family, my husband Marek, and our four children, Adela, Daniel, and our baby twins, Miriam, and Simon.

Love to all of you,

Fannie

Diary, I told Rachel Kaminski the good news, and she offered to have Rivka and the children stay with her. Rachel is not married and lives alone. She says she has plenty of room and would love to have them. Kayla and Jacob will be going to school. She says she can help them to learn English and do their schoolwork.

Chapter 36: Another Death

December 29, 1918

Diary, I received a telegram yesterday and shook while opening it, fearing it was bad news from Vienna, but it was from Sadie. It said, "Itzhak died suddenly late last night. Please come."

I put on my head covering and took the train downtown to Pike Street. On the train, I wondered if the flu killed Itzhak. There is an epidemic of flu, and the health department requires anyone leaving home to wear masks. For reasons no one understands, young men tend to get this flu and die from it.

I knocked, and Sadie opened the door. She looked exhausted. Her eyes were swollen and red from crying. Esther, now almost seven, clung to her mother.

"Sadie, what happened?"

"Yesterday morning, Itzhak didn't feel well. He still wanted to go to shul. I begged him not to go because I knew this was the way the flu starts. You wake up and feel sick. He was always so stubborn. He would never agree to wear a mask, saying if G-d wills him to get sick, wearing or not wearing a mask makes no difference. So, he went. He came home, collapsed, and died within a few hours."

Sadie was trembling. I wrapped my arms around her and soon led her with Esther to the table. I made tea with honey and schnapps. Esther came to me, and I lifted her onto my lap. Sadie put her head in her hands and sobbed. Esther slid off my lap and tried to comfort her mother, "Mama, mama, poor Mama." It was heartbreaking. After a while, Sadie stopped crying and wanted to talk.

"Fannie, we know Itzhak was barely a husband to me or a father to Esther. He only wanted to be a rabbi, and I knew, and maybe he knew too, he could never become a rabbi. He had plenty of knowledge but no wisdom. He could recite what he learned, like a bar mitzvah, but he could never comment on it. He was a tormented soul. I cared for him as one cares for and loves a helpless child. He gave nothing to Esther and little to me, yet he was a part of my life, and I will miss him. Fannie, can you understand?"

"Sadie. You were always compassionate and caring with Itzhak. I can see how you'll miss all you were able to do for him. Because of you he had a much better life than he would have had without you. As for his role as husband and father, you never complained. You showed him respect by your silence, perhaps hoping he could change. Maybe with more time to live, he might have grown wiser. You did all you could to be caring and patient."

"The funeral is tomorrow. Will you and Marek come?"

"We'll be there, and we will be at the shiva too."

The next day, Marek closed the shop for the day, and he and I went to the synagogue on Eldridge Street, across from Feter Oscar's apartment, where I lived when I first arrived in America. It brought back many sad memories as well as memories of the amazing journey to reach my American life as it is now.

Marek went to the men's seats, and I went to the balcony to join the women. I saw Tante Malkah and Zelda, and took a seat next to them. We hugged each other and clasped hands for a few minutes. Many of Sadie's friends from the factory were there. Knowing these women will be there for her in the days ahead comforted me.

The service was long. After, Marek and I shopped for food for the shiva and brought it to Sadie's apartment. There was already a large group crowded into the small space. As I sat there, with Esther sometimes in my lap, or in Marek's or Zelda's, I remembered so vividly how I sat shiva in this room for my sister Esther and my Tateh.

Too many people have died too soon. Fear of losing them always hovers nearby. It takes so much courage to love someone.

Chapter 37: Arrival

March 3, 1919

Diary, today is a momentous day we will never forget. Marek, Adela, Daniel, and I went to Ellis Island to wait for Aber, Rivka, Kayla, and Jacob. The twins stayed with Rachel at our apartment. We thought it important that Adela, age nine, and Daniel, now seven, be with us for the arrival of their aunts and uncles from Europe. They are old enough to remember this miraculous day.

It's hard to believe that nine years have passed since I left the Steamship Neckar in 1910 and spent most of that day on Ellis Island. I was giddy with excitement that day but also frightened and homesick, hoping yet not hoping to be sent back to Europe. I was so naïve to believe that everything in America would be wonderful right away. Over these nine years, I lived through some of my life's worst and best moments. I think I'm about 25 years old now. I hope I have many years ahead.

We gave Aber's name to the official at the front desk so they would be called to meet us as soon as they finished their tests and questions. As far as I knew, they were all well, and since we were vouching for their place to live, it would hopefully go smoothly.

The four of us waited in the reception area near the great hall, sitting on wooden benches. I imagined being once again, a young shtetl girl struggling to make sense of what surrounded me and what I was supposed to do.

Then with a pang, I remembered how Hannah had a big P drawn on her back with chalk, and we thought she was being sent back. I looked at Daniel, my beautiful, red-haired son, and felt tears well up in me for Hannah, but also so much gratitude that Hannah trusted me to be his mother. He is a tender, sensitive boy. I can't imagine my life without him.

Then I remembered Marek, at our first meeting at Sadie's apartment, blessing Daniel; Marek's large hands gently cradling Daniel's little head.

I woke from my memories to hear the loudspeaker, "Will Aber Liebermann and his family come to the reception area." We all stood up, and through the great hall, we saw them, and they saw us. Rivka ran toward us. Aber waved with his cane, but came more slowly. The children stayed by his side. As they came closer, I saw they both looked older and much thinner than I remembered. Rivka looked like a traditional unmarried shtetl woman, with her long brown hair in a braid down her back and dressed in a long skirt and long-sleeved blouse, neat but worn. I was startled to see Mama's face in Rivka. She looks like the Mama I remember as a child. Aber has a lot of gray in his hair and now wears wire-rimmed glasses.

Rivka and I threw our arms around each other, and soon, Aber entered our embrace. The three of us wept, as we kept repeating each other's names as though we were all trying to believe that what was happening at this moment was really happening.

I would never have recognized my little sister and brother. Kayla is 12, small for her age, with large dark eyes that stare out of her narrow face. Jacob, ten, is also small, thin, serious, and wears glasses like Aber. I saw that Jacob had his payes, and that Aber did not.

Marek and all the children were standing by. Finally, we could let go of one another long enough to bring them in.

When I introduced Marek, he embraced and welcomed his adult sister-in-law and brother-in-law, then knelt to greet Kayla and Jacob at their eye level. Adela, nine, in her exuberant way, gave her young aunt and uncle a big hug each, but was shyer with the grown-ups. Daniel, seven, offered a handshake to his two aunts and two uncles.

We all took the train home to the Upper West Side. Rachel was waiting there with Miriam and Simon to greet us. Rachel had prepared tea with fruit and cakes. We all sat around the table, talking, crying, and laughing. Rivka, Aber, and I kept reaching for each other's hands to make sure we were not dreaming.

Rivka, Kayla, and Jacob went home with Rachel, and we planned to all get together again tomorrow. We showed Aber his bed in an alcove in the living room. He lay down on the soft mattress and soon was fast asleep.

What a day this was, a glorious, miraculous day I will never forget.

Chapter 38: Passover

April 14, 1919

Diary, today we celebrated Passover. I can't remember such a joyous seder. Rivka, Rachel, and I cooked all day. Sadie brought her matzoh ball soup, and I made a brisket with carrot, prune, and onion *tzimmes*. For two days, Tante Malkah had a live carp swimming in a basin in her apartment. Today she sacrificed it for the best gefilte fish we ever tasted. She served it with her special horseradish that she grated just before the meal so it would be perfectly fresh and fiery. As she stood over the sink, grating, tears streamed down her cheeks. We teased her, saying this was her way of salting her special horseradish.

Marek went to the Lower East Side to buy Passover matzohs made by the *Lubavitchers.* He said it was something his wife Miriam and he loved to do—get the matzoh just as it came out of the kosher ovens. He took Kayla, Jacob, Adela, Daniel, and Esther with him to see all the frantic running around to make the matzoh according to scripture. The *Lubavitchers* claim it must be done, start to finish, in less than 18 minutes from the first moment water touches the flour to the fully baked, wafer-thin matzoh. Any longer than 18 minutes, and the dough has the chance to rise. They all had the chance to taste the still hot matzoh before carrying the fragile treasure home.

When Marek and the kids returned, I put them to work cutting fruit for a fruit salad while Rivka and I made macaroons.

Rachel had made *charoses* for the seder plate in the Sephardic style. It was new to me. Instead of apples, it was made with dates, almonds, lemon peel, wine, and ginger—so delicious I want to eat it every day all year.

Rachel offered to assemble the ritual plate. She asked Kayla and Jacob to help her. As she placed the hardboiled egg, the roasted bone, the spring greens, and the bitter herbs on the plate along with the charoses, she named each ingredient in Hebrew, then in Yiddish, and finally in English, asking them to repeat after her. At the same time, all three pointed to each food.

I entered the bedroom to put on a new dress I designed and made of soft cotton with a blue floral print, a slim bodice with a V-neck, and a flowing skirt. I slipped into Hannah's shoes which I save for special times. The weather is still cool, so I draped Esther's blue shawl over my shoulders.

We were almost ready to sit down for the Passover seder. We had borrowed extra chairs from our neighbors who were away for the evening, joining their grown children in the Bronx. Marek and Aber lined up three tables and covered them with three white tablecloths so that we had one large table that extended the entire length of the living room.

Marek had a set of Passover dishes, silverware, and wine glasses. He also had six *Haggadahs* for us to share. Marek, Aber, Adela, and Daniel set the table, including a place for Elijah the Prophet. They set out the sweet Passover wine for the adults and grape juice for the children. Jacob brought in the seder plate. I had made several small flower arrangements and set out candles. We were ready.

Marek sat at the head of the table and I sat next to him. Next to me was Rivka, then Aber, Sadie, Tante Malkah, Zelda, Kayla, Rachel, Jacob, Adela, Daniel, and Esther. Miriam and Simon were passed around from one lap to another.

As I looked at this noisy, lively gathering, I felt tears rising and reached for Marek's hand. He squeezed my hand. We looked at each other and laughed. He whispered to me, "Look what we made happen!"

This was all new, and yet I was also, for the moment, swept back to Bolekhiv, sitting with my big family: Mama, Tateh, *Zeyde*, *Bubbe*, and my seven brothers and sisters.

Marek and Aber read the opening prayers sanctifying the feast day, lighting the candles, and blessing the wine. The first glass of wine was poured. They recited the prayers in Hebrew, sometimes stopping to explain them in Yiddish to the children.

After, I walked around the table with a pitcher of water and a small basin, and a towel over my arm so each guest could wash their hands. Marek explained the meaning of the ritual foods in Yiddish. Everyone ate the ritual foods, all complementing Rachel on her delicious charoses. The salt water was explained as signifying tears for all the hardships endured and the green vegetables as the hopefulness of Spring.

From the plate of three matzohs, Aber took out the middle matzoh, snapped it in half, and wrapped it in a napkin. He held it up, showing it to the children explaining it was the *Afikomen*. He handed it to me, telling me to hide it, then told the children they must try to find it later.

Marek poured the second glass of wine. Marek and Aber, back and forth, told the story of the Exodus from Egypt in Yiddish. We sang *Dayenu*.

Marek had coached Daniel to read the four questions in Hebrew. With only a little help, Daniel did a beautiful reading while Aber answered each question.

This was now the time for more questions. Marek asked Aber and Rivka if they were able to celebrate Passover during the war. Aber sighed, saying,

"Before we were sent into the mountains, there were soldier rabbis that came around and led us in reciting the *Kaddish* for those who had died or in prayers of healing for our comrades who were wounded. For Passover, we were on our own. Thankfully, my brothers and I were in the same unit. We put our arms around each other and said the Passover prayers together. When we were in the hospital, a rabbi came around to all the Jewish patients. He had a seder plate with the egg, greens, and bitter herbs. There was also charoses, but nothing like what we have tonight made by Rachel. Those who could get out of bed gathered round the rabbi who led us in the Passover prayers."

Marek asked Rivka, "Did you have Passover in Vienna?"

"When we first arrived in Vienna, we could go with our cousins to the synagogue near us and share Passover with other refugees. As time went on, Jews were often harassed if they were seen going into the shul. So, then we had Passover in our cousins' apartment. Food was very scarce, so the meal was very small. We managed to find some matzoh and apples. I chopped the apples up with some cinnamon for our charoses. When my brothers arrived, Lazar, who had learned to cook in the army, made amazingly delicious roasted cabbage with some dried dill and fried potatoes. Do you remember that meal, Aber?"

Aber nodded and smiled. "Lazar, wherever he chooses to live, will someday be a chef and open his own restaurant."

I came around the table again with the pitcher of water and basin for the second handwashing. We said the blessing over the matzoh, thanking G-d for both leavened and unleavened bread. It was time for our feast!

While those at the table enjoyed the rest of the ritual foods, Rivka, Tante Malkah, Sadie, and I ran back and forth, bringing in the courses. There were cheers for the soup, the gefilte fish, and the brisket.

The children were warned about the horseradish, but the adults screamed with pain and delight as they tasted small amounts along with large forkfuls of gefilte fish. It was good that Rachel had made a huge portion of her wonderful charoses, which was the only thing that seemed to comfort the fire of the horseradish.

I noticed Rachel, sitting between Jacob and Kayla, pointing to all the objects on the table, glasses, plates, tablecloth, candles, and flowers, and saying the names of each in Yiddish and in English. Adela, paying close attention, leaned forward, saying to Kayla and Jacob, "I will help you learn English too. I'm in fourth grade now, and I can speak and write in English."

Then Daniel leaned forward, saying. "I'm in second grade. I can speak English, and I'm also learning to write in English." Esther said, "I can speak English, and I'm very good at arithmetic."

Soon the children were sent to find the Afikomen. Esther was the winner. Aber made sure the matzoh piece she found fit the piece from which it was broken. When it fit perfectly, Aber knelt to be at her eye level and said, "See Esther, things that come apart can sometimes come together again."

It was beautiful to see her smile. Sadie smiled too, so happy to see a cheerful little Esther.

Marek and Aber read the final prayers. Jacob was sent to open the door for the Prophet Elijah. Then we all sang, *L'Shanah Haba'ah B'Yerushalayim.*

The children all left the table to play. The twins were asleep, so Marek and I put them in their cots.

Marek stood up, lifting his wine glass, "First, I want to toast my beloved wife, Fannie, who brings me the deepest joy. She is my love, my partner, and my life's companion in every way."

Marek brought his glass first to my lips and then to his. Then together we drank deeply to the final drop. Marek went on,

"Everyone here is no stranger to hardship. We have all suffered from the cruelties in this world and the deaths of people dear to us. But we are here, now, today at this joyful gathering. We are here to celebrate life, love, and reunion."

More wine was poured, and Aber rose with his glass. "I want to give a special toast to my sister Fannie and her husband Marek, who brought Rivka, Kayla, Jacob, and me out of Egypt, this time called Europe, to join them in America. We all know where we are now is not the end of the journey for the Jews. But it is a welcoming oasis where we heal and refresh ourselves in our quest to live in safety, brotherhood, and peace."

Then I stood and said, "My heart is bursting with joy to see all of you here and together and to remember those we love who have passed. I am here with all of you in the present, and in memory, I re-live our Passover gatherings in Bolekhiv. I find all my past loves living on in each of you, whom I love now."

I paused a moment, feeling nervous about what I wanted to say next. "Soon after Marek and I were married, I went to the library near our apartment and met the librarian, our Rachel, right here. Back then, I called her Miss Kaminski. Rachel has become a cherished friend to Marek, me, and the children. Rachel was intent on helping me to appreciate the English language. After I had visited the library a few times, she and I would sometimes find a quiet corner during her lunch hour and talk. We spoke about our families and our lives. On one visit to the library, she brought me an English poem to study. It was way beyond my abilities at the time, but she encouraged me to persist. I want to read it aloud to you in my heavy Yiddish accent. It is Sonnet 31 by William Shakespeare. It expresses how, even when we lose our beloveds, we find them again in our new loves."

Thy bosom is endeared with all hearts,
Which I by lacking have supposed dead;
And there reigns Love, and all Love's loving parts,
And all those friends which I thought buried.
How many a holy and obsequious tear
Hath dear religious love stol'n from mine eye,
As interest of the dead, which now appear
But things removed that hidden in thee lie!
Thou art the grave where buried love doth live,
Hung with the trophies of my lovers gone,
Who all their parts of me to thee did give,
That due of many now is thine alone:
Their images I loved, I view in thee,
And thou (all they) hast all the all of me.

I was about to offer to read the German translation Rachel had shown me when Rachel stood up. "I'm so happy Fannie read you this beautiful sonnet. I feel like she and I have known each other our whole lives. In a short time, we have shared many of our life stories, and as she said, we have become cherished friends. I knew, by what she told me early on about her family in Europe, herself, and all of you, that this sonnet would speak to her. We lose people we love, but then our new loves often remind us of those we lost. I have taken a big liberty and tried translating this sonnet into Yiddish so all of you can enjoy it."

After Rachel finished reading her Yiddish translation of Sonnet 31, there was a moment of silence, then cheers and applause as we all wiped tears from our eyes. Then Marek said, "It's time to sing. Let's start with *Chad Gadya.*"

We sang many verses, with still many verses to go, when I heard something from the bedroom where the children were playing. It was

Adela's voice, then a whooshing sound, and then gales of laughter from all the kids. I tapped my glass with a spoon and signaled to those at the table to listen.

We all listened, then left the table quietly to peek in the bedroom. There was Adela with her blue and white tablecloth. The kids all held onto it. Then Adela shouted in Yiddish, *"MAKHT MIR DEM HIML!"*

Whoosh! Up went the tablecloth. All the kids ran under it, screaming and giggling as it drifted down onto them. Then again, whoosh! Up went the tablecloth, and Adela now shouted in English, "MAKE ME THE SKY!"

The End

Acknowledgments

Dear Fellow Writers and Readers,

In the spirit of Fannie, I write this letter to all of you. It was Fannie's way of bringing people important to her vividly to mind and engaging with them even in their absence.

Many of you come from the world of psychoanalysis and psychotherapy, but also among you are a health care administrator, chief executive of a human services organization, two scientists, a translator, a writer and editor, and a sociologist. All of you write, in your fields as well as essays, memoir, poetry and fiction. Each of you read the drafts of *Make Me the Sky* bringing to your reading your personal and professional experience, your commitment to the power of the written word to change both the writer and the reader as well as your humanity and curiosity. Many of you are old friends and those of you I didn't know before we shared our writing have become new friends. Reading and commenting on one another's work is an act of trust, bonding, and gratitude. I count it as a rare gift to make new friends in my eighties.

So, thank you dear and trusted friends. You are:

Deanie Blank
David Carlson
Kai Erikson

Tsilia Glinberg

Tim Goldsmith

Linda Gravenson

Peter Hunt

Angelica Kaner

Margaret Mauldon

Stan Possick

Ed Ryan

John Strauss

Marie Zuckerman

And many thanks to the helpful people at *International Psychoanalytic Books* Arnold Richards, Tamar and Larry Schwartz, Noel Morado, Carol Skolnick-Editor, and Kathy Kovacic-Cover Designer.